D0899022

JUDAS GUNS

JUDAS GUNS

Howard Pelham

Walker and Company
New York

RODMAN PUBLIC LIBRARY

B-2

Copyright © 1990 by Howard Pelham

All rights reserved. No part of this book may be reproduced or
transmitted in any form or by any means, electronic or mechanical,
including photocopying, recording, or by any information storage and retrieval
system, without permission in writing from the Publisher.

All the characters and events portrayed in this work are fictitious.

First published in the United States of America in 1990
by Walker Publishing Company, Inc.

Published simultaneously in Canada by Thomas Allen & Son
Canada, Limited, Markham, Ontario

Library of Congress Cataloging-in-Publication Data

Pelham, Howard.
Judas guns / Howard Pelham.
ISBN 0-8027-4104-5
I. Title.
PS3566.E38J84   1990   813'.54—dc20   89-48377

Printed in the United States of America

2   4   6   8   10   9   7   5   3   1

KODMAN PUBLIC LIBRARY

CHAPTER 1

I WAS camped beside a favorite spring of mine in a rugged corner of that area in western Arizona known as Grand Wash Cliffs when the moros mare I was riding at the time, tethered nearby, threw her head up and gazed off toward the south. I took note of that, knowing that if some prowling animal had claimed her attention she would soon return to clipping graze. She didn't, and I got uneasy.

I knew most of the Apaches still loose in the area, and up to a point we were friends. However, I had seen the eyes of some of the younger braves light up when they looked on the mare.

My saddle lay beside the bed of coals which was the remains of my fire. My Winchester, still in its boot, lay beside the saddle. I snaked the Winchester out and faded into some rocks to the north of the camp. I intended to teach any brave that made a move on the mare a lesson he would remember—if that was what it turned out to be—a lesson and a message he would spread among his pals.

Then I heard the singing. Couldn't be anybody but Old Christo Monte. Singing was his special calling card when he wanted to announce his presence to a camp he was approaching. I stepped from the rocks and waited for him to make his appearance.

He came in a few moments later astride old Mary, his grizzled, bony donkey. He pulled her up about twenty yards from my camp and stared at me, his long, thin legs dangling to the ground on either side of the donkey.

1

"You are an hombre who is hard to find, Saxon," he finally said to me.

"Christo, you had about as much trouble finding me as a dog would have sniffing out a bone," I told him. "What brings you into the Cliffs country? Step down and share my camp and coffee."

He slung a leg over the neck of old Mary and stood at her side. The donkey's back didn't quite come up to Christo's belly. Standing there, his pants too short and showing bony ankles, he reminded me of some farmer's garden scarecrow. He wore an old, misshapen felt hat, and it was pulled firmly down on his head. Long, gray hair, surprisingly clean and well kept, fell to his shoulders. His beard, the same quality and color, seemed a part of that cascading hair. All that hair made Old Christo look a little top-heavy.

His face, or that part not covered by hair, was as dark as old leather, and deep, sunken eyes sought out the fire-blackened coffeepot beside the bed of smoldering coals. As he came to the fire, his heavy old six-gun swung almost to his knees. He reached down and pulled the belt up about his waist, but I knew it would soon slip down again. Old Christo didn't have much about his waist to hold it up.

"Don't mind if I do have a little coffee, Saxon," he said as he came up to the fire.

I poured some coffee into two cups and gave Old Christo one. The coffee had been sitting for a while. It was black and thick. I would have apologized to most folks for that black swill, but Old Christo smacked his lips in satisfaction when he looked into the cup.

"Just right, Saxon. Just damned right," he said, and took a swig.

My name is Saxon Younger, and most folks calls me Sax.

I never knew why Christo didn't use the shortened version like everyone else, but I was always Saxon to him.

We squatted on our haunches across the bed of coals from each other and sampled the coffee. Christo smacked his lips again in appreciation. I knew better than to ask him why he had sought me out. Any sign of curiosity on my part would only cause him to stretch the time out until he was ready to speak of it. So I sat there and watched him enjoy the coffee, knowing he would eventually get around to what brought him.

That something had brought him was certain. Old Christo wasn't one to wander into someone's camp just for company. Company he didn't need—nor would he have come to borrow supplies. Like most desert men, me included, Old Christo could have survived on cactus alone, and would have before he'd borrow.

Few men see the desert as a place to exist. Fewer still learn to love it, since the desert can be a lonely place—not to mention the ever-present dangers, dangers that may change with each passing hour. In the desert, windstorms may spring up though the skies are cloudless, stirring up dust so think you can't see two feet before your eyes. Or a water hole you've ridden forty miles to find can go unexplainably dry, leaving you with not enough water to keep a lizard alive. Or the sand dunes may up and shift overnight, changing country you know like the palm of your hand into new and dangerous terrain that must be explored and learned all over again.

And lonely? Well, you don't run into many people in country like that, and some folks find it hard to exist without the company of others. But there are those few who have learned that the danger is nothing more than nature's way of showing a man his weaknesses. If a man can't stand up to that, he needs to cull himself from the desert-seekers, or the desert will do the culling for him. As for loneliness, the best men are those who can stand alone, men who don't hanker after approval and don't need the company of others as a matter of survival. Such men know that the only trustworthy answers are those we mine from within and not from the company of others. I like to think I'm that kind of man. I know for sure Christo Monte is.

"Saxon, I brung you a message from that colonel friend of yours down in Yuma," Christo finally said. "Colonel . . . well, I don't rightly recall his name."

"Piddington? Levi Piddington?" I asked.

"One and the same. Well, this Piddington wanted me to seek you out and give you a message."

Christo drank some more coffee, taking his time. By the time he had got it down, he looked as though he'd forgotten that he had begun to tell me why he had come.

"Well, what's the message, Christo?" I asked.

"Wants you to come down there."

That was all. Not a word about why Levi might want me. Then he stood up as though, his duty done, he was ready to leave.

"Is that all, Christo?" I asked. "Just that he wants me in Yuma? Nothing about why?"

"Why would he tell me that, Saxon?" the old man asked. "It's you he wants down there."

"You mean you rode that donkey halfway across the Territory just to tell me I'm wanted in Yuma with never a word about why? I don't reckon Levi could be very serious. Surely he gave you a hint to pass along, Christo."

"No, nary a hint, Saxon. Though I got the impression he wanted you down there pretty bad." He eyed me speculatively across the coals. "Are you going?"

"That's a long hot ride for a man to take without knowing why he's taking it, Christo. I might just let Levi sweat for five or six months."

He offered me the cup he had used.

"More?" I asked.

"No. No, thank you, Saxon," he answered. "I gotta be going."

He walked to the old donkey, stopped, and turned back to face me.

"Has something to do with a woman, Saxon," he said, "a woman out of St. Louie."

My face must have reflected my astonishment, because I saw a slight smile pass across Christo's face. He enjoyed having saved that thunderbolt until last. And he made no move to leave for the moment—just stood there staring at me, the smile no longer on his face but in his eyes.

"Woman?" I asked incredulously. "What woman? Did Levi say this thing he wants me for had to do with a woman?"

Christo took his time about answering the question, but he finally said, "No, Piddington didn't mention the woman, but she's in town. I know him wanting you down there has something to do with her."

"How do you know that if Levi didn't say it?" I asked.

He gave me a look the implication of which was to ask if I was daft, then threw a bony leg over the donkey and climbed up. He eyed me another moment and said, "I was coming up here anyway. Piddington knew that." Turning old Mary about, he rode north away from my camp.

As for me, I sat there and wondered what a woman in Yuma who was out of St. Louis had to do with Levi wanting me to come there. I didn't question that the two were connected. Christo knew they were, or he would never have said so in the first place. How he came to know that wasn't something he was willing to disclose to me.

A message like that doesn't leave you much choice. I commenced to get ready to travel . . . not that it takes much time for a man like me. I wrapped most of my belongings in rawhide, found a likely spot among the rocks, and cached them, wedging the bundle between two low boulders and piling more rocks on top of them. I didn't want the animals that would come sniffing about my campsite the moment I was gone to be able to satisfy their curiosity. My things would be safe from men, since no one I knew of except Christo and me, and maybe an Indian or two, knew about that spring. Well, if the cache was found, I was leaving only a few things that couldn't be easily replaced.

I took the important things, of course: my Winchester and the old Colt six-gun—a .45, the only handgun I ever owned, and the only one I intended to own unless circumstances beyond my control took it from me. That old six-gun didn't look like much. The metal had dark specks where the rust had wasted the shine away a little, and the bone handles were worn. That just made me value the gun more. I'd never held another gun in my hand that felt more right and natural. Anyone who knows guns and who looked at the business end of the old gun's barrel would know that gun had seen some use over the years, but I won't get into that here.

I took two books with me, the Bible and a copy of Mr. William Shakespeare's plays, wrapping them in limber, soft leather I'd cured myself and stuffed them inside one of my saddlebags. I'm not necessarily a religious man, nor am I a scholar. But I get a lot of pleasure from dipping into those two books from time to time.

In my kind of life, reading is something you can take your time at, and there is no better place to do it than beside a good campfire with the sun going down. You can read a bit and then stare at the sunset as you mull the thoughts over. As much wisdom as the desert offers can be found in those two books if you take your time and dig it out.

Thus equipped, I headed out for Yuma.

CHAPTER 2

ON my first day out of Grand Wash country, I saw I was being followed. The wind had died down about noon, and I saw a thin film of dust hanging against the green on a slope I had come down earlier. Someone was in there among the trees, and they were on the same animal trail I had come down. Of course, I didn't know for sure from that first sighting that it was me they were after. Could be a small party of Indians on the hunt, I reasoned, or cowboys returning from a drive and taking a shortcut. Still, they were back there, and their presence made me nervous.

I kept an eye on them for the next few hours, making a detour off the trail at one spot. They zeroed in on that detour like a bird dog after quail. That left no doubt in my mind I was the rabbit they were chasing.

I had two choices. First, I could pick up my pace and outdistance them. Few men rode horseflesh that could keep up with the moros once I turned her loose. On the other hand, I could drop back and let them come up to me. I could teach them better sense than to hitch onto a gent's trail without knowing who it was they were following. Or maybe they knew. Anyway, I decided they needed the lesson.

I tidied up my trail a bit, leaving only enough sign to keep them from knowing I was on to them, but making it scarce enough that they wouldn't get too suspicious when I wiped it out completely. I also slowed the moros down

8

some so I wouldn't have to double back too far. When darkness fell, instead of going into camp, I turned the mare about.

I caught the flicker of a campfire at once. Strange how careless men can be when they outnumber their quarry and are sure they are the hunters. I guess they'd given no thought to their rabbit turning.

I left the moros in a clump of brush and eased up toward the fire. Their campsite hadn't been picked with wisdom. A screen of rocks flanked the site to the south. I circled to come up behind the rocks and found myself standing within thirty feet of where they sat.

There were three of them, one of whom I recognized at once—Horse Neck McGraw, a Texas badman I'd known once, but with whom I'd never had a run-in. Horse Neck got his name for obvious reasons. He had the longest neck I ever saw on a man: his head appeared to set on a pole, and that feature was the first thing you took note of when you looked at him.

Horse Neck was a big bruiser, and he had put on some heft since I'd seen him last. His brown cord pants circled a heavy belly. His shirt had once been blue. Over the shirt he wore a calfskin vest with splotches that reminded me of the coloring of a pinto pony. The vest hung loose at the sides of his big belly. His hat was Texas-sized, and he wore it pulled firmly down on his head, making it seem even broader and heavier on that long neck.

Horse Neck's nose had been flattened—in a fight, I suppose. The same blow had cost him a couple of front teeth. You couldn't miss that gap when he talked. He had a couple days' growth of beard matching the dark eyes beneath the hat.

I didn't know either of his companions. One was a

ferret-faced little fellow, the kind of man who gives the impression of motion even when he's sitting still. Even there by the fire, as he waited for the coffee to brew and the beans to warm, his eyes kept shifting from side to side. He had a remarkable scar across his left cheek that ran from his temple to his chin. Someone had opened his head up with a sharp knife once. Ferret Face looked a fit companion for Horse Neck.

The third fellow was younger and a different-looking type. By that I mean he didn't have the appearance he was at home in the wild. He wore a black business-type suit and a homburg hat of the same color. The look of meanness hadn't been so firmly stamped on his features, but I'm not one who thinks you can know a book from its cover. A scoundrel can look like a prince, and the other way around as well. Whoever he was, this fellow might put the coarse-featured Horse Neck to shame. However, he did look something of a dude.

I was still convinced that their presence was nothing more than a coincidental encounter—three outlaws, low on funds, coming suddenly on the trail of a single rider. There would always be a horse to sell even if the rider's pockets were empty. That was a logical conclusion under the circumstances, even though the third man wore clothes unlike any hard-riding outlaw I'd ever seen before. A gambler? Down enough on his luck to take up with such a crew? Might be just that.

Curious to learn more, I settled down to wait.

They didn't do much talking until the coffee and beans were served up. Even then they sat back and raked the food in for a time. The dudish one was the first to speak.

"You sure he has no idea we're trailing him, McGraw?" he asked.

"How in hell would he know?" Horse Neck grunted. "We've stayed well back."

"You said he seemed to be slowing up some this afternoon. What does that mean?"

Horse Neck gave the dude a disdainful look. "Well, it don't mean he knows we're back here, Lawson. If he was on to us, you think he'd be slowing down?"

"He was hiding his trail some, Horse Neck," Ferret Face added. "Could be he's caught on. Maybe we should saddle up after we've et and sneak up on his camp and take him."

"He wouldn't have a fire if he knows we're back here, Skittles. How in hell would we find his camp?" That silenced both Lawson and Skittles, but Horse Neck added, "His slowing up don't mean nothing but his horse is wearing down. We'll come up on him tomorrow and take him tomorrow night while he's asleep."

That settled the matter among the three, and they settled down to finish their beans. I backed off from the rocks and circled to come up to where their horses were tethered. The fire cast some flickers even that far out, but none of the three sent a glance in my direction as I loosened the knots and led the horses away. I made the brush where I had cached the moros, climbed into the saddle, and headed south again, leading the three horses behind me.

I turned them loose an hour or so later, confident I had taken them far enough that Horse Neck, Skittles, and Lawson would have to spend a lot of time searching them out. They would fume and curse as they searched, and if they ever found out who it was they had followed, assuming they didn't know already, they would have something to say to me for leaving them afoot in the wild.

A few miles further on I came to a nice little spring

bordered by thick graze. Seemed a likely spot to spend the night, and I did, sleeping soundly, convinced I could do so with no thoughts about Horse Neck and his pards.

Their presence occupied my thoughts some next day. Somehow I couldn't shake the feeling their appearance hadn't been accidental, though I couldn't identify why that thought kept coming back to me. Had they trailed Old Christo into the Grand Wash country knowing he was bringing Levi's message to me? They could have managed that. Christo and old Mary were coming to the age where their senses were letting down some. That being the case, their purpose in taking after me was far more sinister than just a holdup murder. Had the affair something to do with the woman from St. Louis?

I was a few miles from Yuma at the end of the fourth day. Ordinarily, I would make camp and ride in next morning, but I was running low on supplies. Even though I would get there too late to see Levi, there would be time to enjoy a good meal before the cafes closed.

I was the final customer in a little Mexican cantina on the edge of town. The proprietor served me up a Texas-sized steak and some green Mexican beer. The beer couldn't have been more than a day or so old, but the steak made up for that.

But not even a good meal compensates for the way I feel about towns. It's a curbed-in feeling—a feeling that unless I'm real careful I'll bump up against something with no give, something that won't allow me to back off. A strange, weird feeling, which says a lot about me, I suppose. But there it is, and I won't pretend it doesn't exist.

My next stop was at the livery closest to the Paxton House hotel, where I intended to bunk myself. I stayed at the livery until I saw the moros watered, rubbed down, and grained.

That feeling I just described rose up in me real strong as I started along the street to the hotel. I stopped to try and rein it in. A few windows sported lights that watered down the shadows along the street. Two cowboys rode in from the West. They pulled up before the rack at the Cattleman's saloon, tied up, and went in. A half-dozen more horses were tied up there as well. From the saloon came a burst of laughter that drowned out for a moment the sound of a tinny piano. There was the shrill laughter of a woman among the coarser sounds. I thought of the woman from St. Louis who was waiting to see me. I never had a woman waiting to see me before. Such a thing can stir up a man's curiosity.

The Paxton House was a new addition to the town—an addition indicating some of the changes taking place since the government had switched over from the Mexicans. For instance, the Paxton House was a two-story, wood-frame building. Such buildings still looked out of place in the desert, not at all like the adobes that rose from the earth like brown, square toadstools.

"Need a room," I said to the clerk behind the desk.

He was a pale, thin fella—pale skin, pale eyes, pale hair. The blood vessels beneath his skin looked like blue spiderwebs. He wore glasses, which caught the glare from a chandelier overhead, and I failed to catch the question in his gaze.

"Would you be Sax Younger?" he asked, taking me by surprise.

"I would be," I answered back.

"In that case, I have a room waiting for you. Been ready for a few nights now. Colonel Piddington came in and reserved it. Paid for it, too."

He turned the register around and pushed it toward

me, pushing a pen at me as well. I signed. He gave me a key.

"Up the stairs," the clerk said. "It's the corner room, and it'll be on your left."

Levi had been mighty all-fired sure I would come, I thought to myself as I stood there. Then I thought of Christo's parting shot. Levi knew Christo as well as I did. Had he been sure Christo would drop that about a woman on me, making the bait one he knew I couldn't resist?

"You got a woman from St. Louis staying here?" I asked the clerk.

He gave me a cautious look, as though he wasn't sure he should give out such information. But he changed his mind and said, "Mrs. Dupard. Janna Dupard. She's been here two weeks."

The longer I wander the desert country the shier I become in the company of women who aren't of a certain type. I guess having a name for the mystery woman made her come to life for me. I found myself getting flustered. That clerk didn't help matters, either.

"You know Mrs. Dupard?" he asked.

Unable to think of a word to say, I just picked up my bedroll, saddlebags, and Winchester, and made for the stairs. On the upper floor I went along a lamplit corridor and found the room. Inside, I dumped everything on the bed and crossed to a bureau, on which sat an oil lamp. I struck a match and lit it, then closed the door. Standing before the door, I wrestled again with the feeling of being closed in. Getting it under control, I crossed to the window.

CHAPTER 3

THE window opened on the street, and just below was the roof of the hotel's front porch. The window was easily reachable from there. I ran my fingers along the window frame and searched for a lock, and found that there wasn't one. That left me feeling uneasy again.

The window faced the south, and way off down there were a few clouds still faintly dusted with red from a sun long beyond the horizon. A few stars were out, but they seemed more distant and smaller hanging over a town. Stars over a town don't seem a part of things.

Stars look different in the desert. In the desert you know they have their place in the scheme. Night in the desert has a way of pulling things together, showing the proper relationships. The light is a part of it, a light that doesn't seem to come altogether from the moon and the stars, but out of all desert things. The light links up and makes a cactus and even the stars seem to belong together.

In a town? Well, in a town things are different.

From the window I could see the hitch rack of the Cattleman's, though not the front of the saloon. More riders kept coming and tying up. The noise from inside increased as the crowd built. I'm not much of a drinking man, which may be because I seldom find myself close enough to a town to visit a saloon. But I've never minded nursing along a shot of good rye whiskey when the opportunity was there. I guess that's why I found my way back downstairs and walked to where all the noise was coming

15

from. Or maybe I thought in that crowded place the walls wouldn't feel as close.

They were whooping it up when I eased in there. Sprinkled about the room were a half-dozen decked out doves—soiled doves, some call them. They didn't even manage to look bawdy in their feathers and other finery. One looked head and shoulders above the rest. She had bright hair, and her lowcut gown offered up creamy shoulders and a tempting bosom. She extracted the tinny sounds from an upright piano, and I counted eight men gathered about the piano and her. Card games occupied men at tables in the rear. Other tables were circled by men who had dropped in for a drink and talk, or to fondle the women, maybe even take them upstairs. The women were obliging. With the exception of the one at the piano, they circulated from table to table. The bar seemed the least busy place of all. I walked to it, propped a foot on the brass rail, and waited to order my drink.

The bartender, seeing me, moved down to where I stood. He was a fancy dresser with a horse-sized girth. Over black serge pants he wore a white apron, but his shirt was where the fanciness came in. It was varicolored as a rainbow, the stripes running up and down. At his throat was a white bowtie, and he wore broad white suspenders.

He had a walrus mustache whose part was centered very accurately beneath his nose. I skipped the other features of his face and let my eyes travel up to his head. His hair, of the exact color of his mustache, was parted on a line with the part in the mustache and was swept back in the identical way, duplicating the mustache but much oversized. All that hair gave his face a squat look, and I found myself concentrating on the lines in his hair.

"What'll it be?" he asked.

"A shot of rye—if it's good," I said.

He measured me with a look. Making up his mind, he took a couple of steps along the bar, reached beneath it, and took a bottle out. He actually blew some dust from it before he opened it up and poured my drink.

"Won't find any better than that," he said, placing the shot glass before me.

I gave it the test, nodded my agreement, and settled down to enjoy some good rye whiskey. For a few moments the sound of the piano, the laughter, the hum of talk, even the walls receded. For those moments I concentrated on the drink, forgiving the bartender even his strange appearance. The quality of that rye lived up to the dust on its bottle, and I had a refill.

I was ready to leave when from behind me came the sound of others entering. I glanced into the mirror behind the bar and saw Horse Neck, Skittles, and Lawson, along with a fourth. All four searched the room with hard eyes, obviously on the lookout for someone.

I figured I knew who they were looking for. The only question in my mind was whether they'd know it was me. They concentrated on the crowded room and appeared to ignore the bar. They even took a few steps forward. I made up my mind to try and slip behind them if they moved in far enough. That proved a wishful thought, because Horse Neck turned and looked directly at me.

"By God, men! There he is!" he shouted. "Let's take him now!"

He grabbed for leather. The other three, turning as one, did the same.

That didn't leave me much choice. A moving target is the hardest to hit, so I launched myself in a somersault along the floor, grabbing for the old Colt as I rolled.

Behind me, and in the midst of the explosions, I heard their bullets walking a splintered path across the planks as they followed me. The thuds had a deadlier sound than the bang of the guns.

I ended my roll and came up shooting. By now Horse Neck was no more than ten feet away. I caught a quick glance at him as he stood there triggering his gun. His face was flushed with the lust to kill. He took my bullet in his chest and was spun around by it. As he fell face down on a table, he and the table skidded a few feet across the floor.

The gunfight brought pandemonium to the saloon. I was only vaguely aware of that, of course, but somewhere back there my mind registered the screams of the women, the crashing of a table overturned to provide cover, and among all that I couldn't hear the piano anymore. I got off a shot at Skittles, but missed. His bullet smashed into a chair before me as I snaked my way behind a table someone had upturned. Then a shotgun blast exploded above everything else.

I couldn't remember seeing a shotgun in the hands of any of the four, but that didn't mean they didn't have someone already in the saloon to back them. They had proved themselves resourceful enough to catch their horses and almost beat me to Yuma. A shotgun backup was no surprise at that moment.

I eased my head above the edge of the table. My intent was to locate that shotgun and take it out before it was turned on me in earnest. It was in the hands of Walrus Face behind the bar, but it wasn't turned on me. Instead, it was pointing toward the ceiling. He pulled the trigger again, and the blast drowned out everything else again. Satisfied I had nothing to fear from that source, I turned back to the three gunmen left standing—just in time to see them crash through the Cattleman's swinging doors and onto the street. Lying there behind my table, I listened for and heard the sound of running horses pound away down the street and into the night.

A minute or so passed, and there wasn't a sound to be heard in the saloon. As I stood up, me and the bartender were the only ones to be seen. Then other heads began to pop up. I watched as at least a dozen came from behind the piano.

I had some questions I needed to put to Horse Neck McGraw, so I walked over to the table where he lay and rolled him over. If he was still alive, I intended to ask him how he came to take up my trail—and if there was more to it than just a holdup and murder, and the pride-hurting fact of being left afoot in the wild. But Horse Neck, whose actual name was Henry, would talk no more. He stared open-eyed up into the saloon at the spot where the bartender's shotgun blast had hit the ceiling. His mouth hung open a full two inches. That gaping hollow seemed to express disbelief at what had happened.

"Drop that gun, stranger!" a voice behind me commanded, "Or I'll plug you where you stand!"

I was still standing over McGraw, the old Colt in my hand. That order didn't sound like one to argue with. I eased back from the table and let the gun drop to the floor. Turning, I faced the speaker.

He wore a marshal's badge, and he looked like a no-nonsense kind of lawman, a tough, rangy-looking type. His eyes might have been ice, and I didn't see anything about him that looked edgy—just ready.

"Liston," he said, his voice indicating that was his name. "I hope you got a good reason for shooting a man down in my town."

"Best reason of all," I answered. "I shot him down before he could do the same for me—not that he didn't get the chance to try."

The bartender came forward, the shotgun still in his hands.

"Is he being truthful, Jackson?" Marshal Liston asked. "Did the man lying dead shoot first?"

"That's the way it was, Marshal." Jackson replied. "Took one look at this gent, yelled, and drew his gun. There were four of them. They all got off some shots. This fella is lucky to be alive. Wouldn't be, I guess, if he hadn't sprouted wings."

"Sprouted wings?" the marshal asked.

"Yeah, he sort of launched himself through the air with the bullets of those four tracking him. Got off a shot in midair, or so it seemed. This fella there took that first bullet and went down. Never seen shooting like that before. Like the lead had a homing device for its target. I stepped in then with Betsy. Got the attention at once of the three that were left. They dashed out of here before you came in."

"They almost ran over me," the marshal said. "I thought they were just getting away from the gunplay." He turned to me. "Who might you be, mister, who can attract all this trouble?"

"Younger. Sax Younger."

The marshal's squint tightened a little. That told me he had heard the name. I didn't feel at all happy about that. Some wild stories circulate about me. You know how it is. People take a smidgen of truth and add a lot more from their imaginations. They come up with yarns that stretch the truth a mile. I hoped Marshal Liston hadn't been told stories like that.

"The fella from the desert," he said. "Used to do some scouting for the Army."

"That's me. I learned to prefer the wide open spaces," I said.

"A little partial to them myself at times," Liston replied. "But I reckon you better tell me what you know about this man and what was behind this attack."

"His name is Henry McGraw. I saw him a few times down in Texas. Wasn't one to let the law hold him back much. Most folks knew him as Horse Neck. You can see why if you take a look at that long neck.

"Why they were after me I can't say. Got on my trail four days north of here in the Grand Wash country. I doubled back to find out what their purpose was. All I found out was that they had murder on their minds. I thought they just wanted the poke I was carrying—that they didn't know and didn't care who I was. I sneaked off with their horses and left them afoot. How they got here almost as soon as I did, I'm still trying to figure out."

"Maybe they got a look at you up there and recognized you when they walked in here."

"Maybe," I said.

I wasn't about to mention my reason for riding into Yuma. As far as I knew, whatever Levi had in mind might need to be kept secret.

"I guess that explains everything for now. Leaving me afoot like that would make me mad enough to begin shooting when I next saw the gent, I guess. You can pick up your gun, Younger. But I want no more trouble. We're running a peaceful town here now. I want that understood."

"It's clear as a bell on a cold morning, Marshal," I said. "I just hope you'll get that message to the other three."

"When'll you be riding out?" he asked.

"I'll be here a day or two, Marshal—if that's all right with you."

Without answering he turned and left the saloon.

"Maybe you'd like another shot of that rye whiskey before you go?" Jackson asked.

"You, my friend, are a mind reader," I said. "I need to thank you for stepping in on my behalf. Maybe saved my skin."

"Nothing to thank me for. A man who enjoys good rye whiskey can't be all bad, I always say. I'm glad I did for another reason, too," he added.

"What could that be?" I asked.

"Well, I know the name. The name of Sax Younger is a bit of a symbol for some. Stands for a lot of what's best out here. Hope that don't embarrass you none."

Well, it did, so I just didn't answer. He brought the dust-covered bottle back out, pouring two drinks this time.

"This one is on the house," he said. "And I'll have a nip with you if that's all right with you."

"Nothing could be more fit," I answered, and we lifted a glass to each other.

I didn't linger in the Cattleman's—didn't seem the prudent thing to do with those three on the loose and knowing where I was. With the rye feeling warm in my belly, I left the saloon and returned to my room.

The bed, with its two mattresses and springs, proved too soft for me. I kept bouncing up and down when I did no more than turn. Each breath I took got a squeaking response from the springs as well. That seemed a far cry from being lulled to sleep by desert sounds.

Maybe my discomfort was enhanced by a very important unanswered question. Were all the attentions I had received from Horse Neck McGraw and the others connected with why Levi had summoned me to Yuma? There was no proof thus far that there was, but I couldn't shake the feeling that there had to be. Maybe Levi would be able to throw some light on the matter come morning.

Eventually, I remembered that window with no lock, and how easy it would be for someone to gain entrance from the porch. That got me to thinking, so I took a blanket and spread it in the shadows along a wall. I went to sleep cuddling the old Colt.

CHAPTER 4

DAWN had crept into the room when I awoke. I lay still for a moment and got my bearings. The old Colt was still resting on my chest. That put things into focus for me. I pushed myself up, stretched cramped muscles, and crossed over to the window.

The street was deserted. From the East, a blood-red sun had inched its way into view. A string of clouds, some with dark bases, hung between me and the sun. Somewhere, someone might get rain, a sight always welcome in desert country.

Retreating from the window, I took time to swab myself down with a cloth, using water from the porcelain pitcher and pan on the bureau. I shaved and dug out some fresh clothes. I was dressed and thinking of breakfast when the knock came. My hand on the butt of the old Colt, I opened the door.

Levi Piddington stood there. We eyed each other for a long moment, each taking in the familiar face of the other. I hadn't seen Levi in several months, and something about him looked different—something I couldn't quite put my finger on. It wasn't physical—more intangible than that, something about the way he faced me, maybe a less certain look in his eyes.

He was small and wiry. Despite his size, no officer ever carried himself with more military bearing. His back was ramrod straight, his shoulders thrown back, his uniform, now as ever, creased and spotless. But somehow that stiff military look didn't seem quite as convincing as it always had before.

He held his hat in his hand, and I looked at his close-cropped hair. Once black, it was brindle now. That hadn't been true the last time I had seen him, and something had chased his hairline back from his forehead a little.

Piercing dark eyes and black brows—no brindle there yet—dominated his face. Hollow cheeks gave his face a longer look, and his prominent nose was less so. When he smiled, as he did now, his lips parted to expose an even line of fine teeth. He was forty-three, thirteen years older than I was. Somehow, for the first time that I could recall, he looked older.

"By God, Sax!" he said. "Took you long enough to get here!"

He grabbed my outstretched hand, and we shook. As usual I was surprised at the strength in a hand I could wrap my own around.

"If you'd send me a regular message, Levi, instead of giving it to Old Christo, I might have got here sooner. Takes Christo a month of Sundays just to cross the Territory. Old Mary isn't as spry as she once was."

"Neither am I, Sax," he said. "Neither am I. Anyway, if you'd settle in some place like a civilized man, it wouldn't be so hard to get word out to you. When I asked Christo where you might be found, he just waved a hand vaguely about and told me some place out there. That's as close as I could come to an address."

"How about me buying an old friend some breakfast?" I asked.

"Not on your life! I've been ordered to bring you home. Amanda is busy right now cooking up something for us. She'd have my scalp if I didn't show up with you. She's been planning her campaign for weeks to get you hitched to some nice gal here in town. Got three or four lined up, I understand. Some are worth branding, Sax. 'Course, I ain't had no hand in it, but I can't help but hope one will catch your fancy. Be nice to have you among us again."

I didn't answer. Amanda had put some energy into such efforts before. She always managed to trot out a nice churchgoing girl or two when I was about. I never minded much. She was just mothering me. I had little fear that such a girl would ever get interested in me. What woman would want thus to be saddled? A man with no roots, whose chief hankering is forever to be on the move, searching out places most men prefer to shun. A man that other men were sometimes on the prowl for. What woman would want to hook up with a man like that?

And me settled in a town? The very thought made me want to feel the sides of the moros between my knees. I guess Levi sensed that, because he suddenly laughed.

"Well, come on," he said. "Let's get on to breakfast."

We went downstairs, outside, and along the street toward Levi's house. The sun had put some space between itself and the horizon. Already the heat was building. I found myself longing for the fresh winds and the solitude of the Grand Wash country.

"How did you know I'd got in, Levi?"

He gave me a look. "You got to be kidding. After that ruckus last night, everyone in Yuma knows you've arrived."

There was distinct disapproval in Levi's voice and the look he gave me. The gunfights I seemed always drawn into were a touchy subject between us. I think the way Levi felt about them was part of what sent me into the desert. Not all, and I've talked about that some already. It was Levi's contention I brought them on those gunfights—that something about me, something in my air that was broadcast to other men, carried a dare. I have puzzled over that long and hard. Maybe he was right. Maybe when any man takes charge of his own space, it's a dare to other men. It's a sign that they have to go around and not through. In the Territory at the time there were men who would take that as a challenge.

But there was more to it than that, something I had never confessed to Levi. There was something in me—the same thing as was in other men—something that liked the challenge, the nearness of death, and that split second when you fought to ward it off or you would have to embrace it, that I responded to. I had some fear of embracing death, and I wasn't proud of it. And though I had never confessed it to Levi, it was there.

"Last night was no fault of mine, Levi," I said.

"That's what Travis Liston said when he reported to me that you were in town. He dropped by last night after he saw you go to your room. I had asked him to keep an eye out for you. Told him you were tamed. He disputed that some. What was the shooting about, Sax?" he asked.

I figured Liston had already given him the official version. Levi was probing for more. Maybe he wanted to judge whether I had changed or not.

"The thought occurs to me, Levi, it has something to do with why you sent for me. I spied those hard cases on my tail soon after I left Christo. Could they have followed Old Christo to me? Is there some reason someone might not want me to get to Yuma? Could that be true, Levi?"

He thought about it for a moment, seeming to consider the possibility seriously.

"There couldn't be any connection, Sax," he finally said. "There isn't anything sinister or secret about why I sent for you. No reason whatever for someone to try and keep you from coming in."

"Well, I did steal their mounts and leave them afoot. I guess that stirred them up enough to send them after me."

Levi laughed. "I'd chase after you myself if you did that to me. I don't think I'd draw on you though, Sax. You're too good. Sometimes I've wished you weren't."

"Are you saying you'd like to see me take a bullet, Levi?" I asked. That was the sense of what he had said, but I couldn't believe he meant it.

"No. Not that, of course. But if you weren't so damn fast with that gun, maybe you'd invite less trouble—go out of your way a little. You'd live longer. Someday you won't be quite fast enough. I think of that day. I don't want to see it come, my friend. But it will. Someday it will come."

His voice had a dark, brooding sound—like he carried that image in his mind—had lived with it for some time. I didn't know what that was a sign of. But Levi sounded sad—sad and sorrowful. On the street a store here and there had opened up. Proprietors stared at us as we passed, through dust-encrusted, barred windows. When there were no windows, they stepped to their doors. They seemed to wonder what had brought Colonel Piddington out so early.

"Why did you send for me, Levi?" I asked.

For a moment he seemed to collect his thoughts. Then he said, "Do you recall a raid on a stagecoach involving a rich fella from St. Louis about three years back? He was traveling with his six-year-old son. The man, along with the rest of the passengers and driver, was killed in the raid. Their bodies were found on the scene. They had been scalped. Some of them pretty well mutilated. But the boy's body wasn't found. And he was never heard from again—that is, until recently."

"Was that man's name Dupard?" I asked.

Levi shot me a glance. "You do remember then, don't you?"

"Some," I said. "But Christo dropped something about a woman from St. Louis on me. I asked the clerk at the hotel about such a woman. He gave me the name."

Levi smiled and said, "I knew Christo would figure it all out. You'll be meeting the lady later this morning."

"Why?" I wanted to know.

"She is the boy's mother. She's out here to organize a search for him."

"Even if he's alive, Levi, I'm not sure the Apache would give him up. I'm not sure the boy would want to leave after three years. In that length of time, they'll have turned him into one of them."

"Turns out the raid wasn't made by Apache, Sax," Levi said.

"Not Apache? Who then?"

"Serona," he answered.

For a moment that meant nothing to me. Then something in the back of my mind stirred, and I remembered the name. The Serona were more legend than anything else. They were a seldom mentioned tribe deep in the Sonoran Desert of Mexico. Stories were told of even the Apache shunning their land.

"Never heard of them ranging this far north." I said.

"Nor me," Levi said. "But Janna Dupard offers some convincing evidence they did. She has come up with a witness that the Serona have the boy."

"Who?"

"A fella by the name of Baxter Logan. Owns a ranch

that borders the desert down there. Says he hires a Serona from time to time as vaquero. Seems he heard them discussing a raid once—and the boy that was taken."

"How did Janna Dupard happen to latch onto him?" I asked.

"She didn't find him. He came to her. Turned up in St. Louis and sought her out to give her the word. Apparently, the Dupards checked out his story and believe it to be true. Campost Dupard—that's the boy's grandfather—is a very powerful man and richer than Croesus. He pulls strings that reach all the way to Washington. He's very sick—maybe on his deathbed. He is determined to know if his grandson is alive or dead before his time comes. I have been ordered to give his daughter-in-law every assistance. I sent for you because I don't know of anyone better equipped to lead a small party in and out of that desert."

"Small party? You'll need a regiment when the Serona get wind you're coming."

"Sax, the Army has nothing to do with this," Levi said. "The Mexican government will not even be told. That's why the group must be kept as small as possible . . . in order to look very innocent if it stumbles into a Mexican Army patrol. In fact, there will be only three people."

"Three? Me and who else?" I asked, my voice reflecting my disbelief that Levi could be serious.

"Mrs. Dupard will be one," he said calmly.

He was expecting the response that he got from me, and he waited for it to come, a slight smile cracking his thin lips. I didn't keep him waiting.

"You can't be serious, Levi," I said. "No woman in her right mind would consider such a trip. That's some of the roughest country on the continent. Not only is it desert, it's mountainous. Men hardened to desert travel have gone in there and never come out again. A pampered rich lady from St. Louis wouldn't survive a week. You should have made that clear to her."

"Oh, I did, Sax. I explained everything, described the country, showed her some similar terrain on a topographical map. She brushed it all aside. I have about come to the conclusion that if any woman can stand up to such hardships this one can. She's tough, Sax. She may not strike you as such in the beginning, but I've spent some time with her. She is determined to go in and get the boy. Never underestimate the grit a mother's love can provide to an effort, Sax."

"Never mind her grit," I said. "Can she ride? And for how long? And how long can she go without water? Does she handle a gun? If so, would she be willing to use it if the Serona don't extend us welcome. Which they won't is my likely bet. I expect you didn't cover all that with her, did you, Levi?"

"I did, Sax." He looked up at me and smiled indulgently. "You'll see for yourself. We're to meet her at my office after we've had breakfast. I asked her to bring Logan along. I thought you'd want to talk with him. Richard Farley will likely accompany them. He has dogged her footsteps since she's been here."

"Who is Farley?" I asked.

"A friend of the family—actually, Yancey Dupard's friend. Yancey was the boy's father. Farley and Young Dupard grew up together. I gather from a few words Farley has let slip that he is terribly in love with his friend's wife—maybe even before she married Yancey."

"Is Farley to be the third party in the group then?" I asked.

"No, Farley isn't going. He plans a return to St. Louis as

soon as he sees the expedition off. Seems there is pressing business awaiting him there."

That sounded farfetched to me. What man who was in love with a woman would agree to let her go off into the desert to seek out wild Indians and not be with her? Didn't make sense to me, but I'd never traveled much in the company of the rich.

"We have now eliminated Logan and Farley from the party, Levi," I said. "But you still haven't told me who is to be the third member. Why are you stalling?"

He gave me a pleased look. "I have decided to traipse along with you myself, Sax. What do you think of that? We haven't traveled the desert together for years. I just can't resist the temptation of one more time out there. Besides, I can't rightfully send you down there to face what might turn out to be a real hostile bunch and not go along myself."

"It's been a long time since you were out there, Levi," I said. "I know you stay in shape, but . . ."

"Don't hand me that line, Sax Younger!" he snapped. "I'll stay up with you and any man any day of the week. You know that as well as I do."

I did know it, and I asked, "How about Amanda? What does she think of your going?"

"Well, I have to confess she isn't happy about it, but she has given me her blessing—that is, if you accept the job."

"Since when did you start asking her permission?" I asked.

"This isn't Army business," he said. "Since it isn't, she has a right to a say. And those are her terms."

"What?"

"That you take the assignment. Otherwise, she says she won't hear of me going. 'Course, I don't tell you that to pressure you."

"Oh, no!"

"No."

"I'm to believe that if I say no to Mrs. Dupart you won't be making the trip, either? Is that correct?" I asked.

"That's the agreement I have with Amanda, and I'll stick with it," he said.

I left it at that, and we came to the house. Amanda must have seen our approach from inside. She met us halfway down the walk. She stood before me a moment, her arms outstretched for an embrace, as she looked me over.

"Just give me a nice long look, Sax," she said. "These eyes have long been aching for the sight."

"You haven't changed a whit, Amanda," I said. "Still the most beautiful woman in the Territory. Give me a hug."

Her arms reached up for my neck as mine circled her waist. Levi beamed his approval.

She had changed, though. The years had deepened the lines in her face, and those at the corners of each eye gave her a continuous squint, or seemed to. Those seemed to be fresh worry lines. Amanda wasn't as consenting as Levi thought to this trip. Or else something else was wrong.

Her hair had grayed more, giving her something of a faded look that wrenched at me. Her brown eyes still retained their sparkle, however, as she peered up at me. The sparkle didn't hide a certain look, though. I had seen that look before, or one very nearly like it, each time Levi had ridden off to fight the Apache. Now he was riding out again. Was Amanda again feeling the fear of seeing her man ride off into battle? I couldn't quite believe it. There was something other than just fear.

She rushed us into the house and to her table, where more food than a half-dozen men could eat was waiting. She sat with us and nibbled, but only occasionally. Either she had already had her breakfast, or whatever was bothering her had stolen her appetite.

Levi seemed unaware of the strain in Amanda as he attacked the food. Was he too close to her to see how much she was affected? For the first time ever some question of Levi's love for Amanda entered my mind.

"What else do you know of the Serona, Sax?" Levi asked.

I didn't like discussing the Serona in front of Amanda, but there seemed nothing I could do about it.

"Not much, Levi," I said. "There is that yarn about them shooting silver bullets. Supposed to be the only metal they have access to. I never believed such tales, though."

"Why not?"

"I always figured that was like all the other tales of treasure. You know . . . all the gold and silver mines once worked by the Spanish, but for some unknown reason closed up and left behind, their locations long since lost in time. Like the Seven Cities of Cebola. That legend of golden cities occupied the Spanish for years. Cost them an army or two. They never found anything but a few poor Indian villages. I expect the Serona silver amounts to about the same thing.

Levi didn't say whether he agreed with my assessment or not. Instead, he asked, "What else do you know about them?"

"That their numbers are small, but that they can be as fierce, or fiercer, than the Apache, that they occupy some valley in the heart of a mountain range where the Sonoran Desert gets the hottest. I guess that about covers it."

"Hmmm . . ." Levi said, appearing to think it over.

"Do you know more?" I asked.

"I know what Janna Dupard says she has found out about them. It doesn't agree with what you've said, except that the silver does seem to exist, though her source doesn't mention a large amount."

"Who is her source? Logan?" I asked.

"No, a Spanish priest who lived among the Serona a century or so ago. Logan located the priest's manuscript in the Church archives in Mexico City. Brought a copy along to St. Louis. I'll let Mrs. Dupard tell you of the contents."

"This Logan's had a hand in this affair from start to finish, Levi. Who is he anyway?"

"He is an American who has lived in Mexico a few years," Levi answered. "I believe I told you he owns a ranch down there."

"How did he come to locate in Mexico?"

"He's an ex-Confederate—a major. Fled there after Lee surrendered."

"I'm not sure I like the sound of that," I said. "Some of those boys still have axes to grind."

"Apparently, Logan isn't one of those," Levi replied. "Mrs. Dupard says she had Allan Pinkerton check him out thoroughly. Besides, I can't hold running off to Mexico against him. If we had lost, I might have wound up in Canada."

Amanda had listened to our talk with downcast eyes. I knew now that Levi had no inkling of how much this last fling of his was affecting her. For that was what it was, I told myself, a final campaign, though the command would consist of only the three of us, before he wound up behind some civilized desk back East somewhere. Perhaps he had come to accept the fact that there would be no more battles for him, no more campaigns in which to win honor and promotions. Too much peace had broken out on the frontier now. That's the way it is with soldiers. Advancement depends upon the very things wives and sweethearts fear the most—the battles.

"Well, we must be off," Levi said, pushing back from the table. He stood and took a gold watch from his waistcoat pocket. "We'll barely make it to the Paxton House by the time I told the lady we would call on her."

He went to Amanda and embraced her, planting a kiss on her lips. I was happy to see that, and I felt a little ashamed of my previous doubts of his love. Amanda and Levi were a team. I couldn't imagine them not together.

"I'll bring him home for lunch, sweetheart," Levi said.

"I'll cook something special for you, Sax," she said.

She followed Levi around the table, stopping by me and taking my arm, as Levi left the dining room. I read the pressure in her hand and stayed beside her.

"I suppose you'll go," she said.

"I haven't made up my mind," I answered. "I don't intend to until I have met the lady."

Amanda frowned. "I wish I could say you won't like her, Sax—that she's a foolish, rich woman so lacking in judgment she'll risk her own life and the lives of others to follow a whim. But I can't tell you that. The truth is she is a remarkable woman, a strong woman. Most of all she is a woman who grieves for her child. Oh, not openly, with tears in her eyes. But her grief is real. You'll see it. It'll win you over, as it did Levi. I never had a child, but as a woman I share her grief. She keeps thinking of that boy in the hands of savages. She keeps wondering what is happening to him. It's in her head always, asleep or awake. Despite all that, she keeps asking herself if he's still alive."

Tears welled into Amanda's eyes. I had known for a long time of her inability to have children. There had been a time, I knew, when her barrenness had seemed to bring

Levi and her even closer. Had that changed? Was that what put the look in her eyes—that troubled me so? But why, suddenly, would that make a difference between them? It didn't make sense.

"Is there something wrong, Amanda? Something you don't think you can speak to me of?" I asked.

That stricken look deepened for an instant. She glanced to the doorway through which Levi had disappeared. She had the urge to tell me. That much I could see, but it passed as quickly as it had arisen.

"Just take care of him, Sax. See that he comes back."

"Me take care of Levi?" I joked. "The man who taught me most of what I know? He'll wind up looking out for me."

"No, Sax. I—I have this feeling. This—this terrible dread. I can't explain it beyond that."

She might not be able to explain it, but the feeling was obviously very real to her. Suddenly, her face seemed to have aged by ten years.

"Would you like for me to tell the lady I won't go?" I asked her.

"Would you not go if I answered yes?"

"I won't budge if you give me the word."

She was tempted—sorely, sorely tempted. I could see as much in her eyes. She squeezed the look off, however.

"No, I can't do that to him," she said after a moment. "I'm sure he'll tell you, if he hasn't already, that our rotation will soon come around. We'll be shipping out for the East very soon. I believe Levi looks on this as his last chance to see action out here—that and his last chance to be with you. I can't deny it to him. Besides, if you're along, he'll come back to me. I know he will."

"I may decide on my own not to go," I said.

"No, Sax, you'll go," she said. "One look at Janna Dupard's face and you'll have no choice. I know you too well. Just promise me one thing."

"Anything that is in my power to give, Amanda."

"Bring him back. Bring yourself back."

"Both," I said. "I promise you both."

My voice almost cracked with the surge of emotion that welled up in me for this woman whose love for me was too deep for me to fathom. I took her in my arms and held her close for a second. She broke the embrace, stepping back.

"Enough of such talk," she said, forcing some cheer into her voice. "I'm planning a party for you. I'm inviting all the eligible ladies. Maybe I can get you married off. That would put a stop to your wanderings, or make it harder for you anyway. Does that frighten you so much?"

"Not at all—not if another like you turned up in the bunch, but I have a suggestion."

"What?"

"Wait till we get back. We'll celebrate our return and make it a farewell celebration for you and Levi. We'll invite half the Territory."

"You see! You've already made up your mind to go, haven't you?" she said. "And you're just putting me off. You're afraid I'll introduce you to a normal, home-loving girl you'll like so much you won't be able to turn your back on her. I know that very well, but I'll agree to wait under one condition."

"Which is?"

"You'll stay right here in the house with Levi and me for several days. You'll sit down to tea with whoever I invite and get to know them. That you'll invite them for long buggy rides in the moonlight. Do you agree?"

I shuddered, but I said, "Sounds like heaven on earth to me."

She tiptoed to plant a kiss on my cheek. "You're a handsome devil, Sax Younger," she said. "Those blue eyes turn a woman's stomach to jelly."

"And you, my sweet, are a born liar who does and says everything she can to embarrass me. If you weren't tied up with Levi, I'd tie you behind me on my trusty steed and ride off into the desert with you."

Levi stuck his head in. "When you're finished flirting with my wife, boy, we'd best be on the move."

CHAPTER 5

OUTSIDE, the sun was putting its brand on the street. The hard-packed clay looked drier, and it bounced the heat and the glare into our faces. The wind was from the South, and there was the feel of an oven to it. There was just the hint of the heat of hell in that wind. More than ever I wished myself out of Yuma and in the hilly country again. I knew the turmoil in Amanda had something to do with that.

Levi gave me a look. His mind didn't seem to be on the heat. Had he overheard some of what Amanda had said?

He must have, because he said, "Don't get yourself all worked up over Amanda's talk, Sax. Women get like that when they reach a certain age. Things happen in their bodies. They get insecure. Any change, even for a short time, seems like a calamity."

"That's all it is?" I asked.

"What else could it be? Why she even acts a little suspicious of me. You have to use patience with her."

"Maybe you should give up going on this trip, Levi."

He was silent. We walked a half a block.

"I have considered it," he finally said. "My going, of course, depends on what you decide. But assuming you take Mrs. Dupard's offer, I have made up my mind to tag along. Eventually, Amanda would feel even worse if I didn't. You know how she is, Sax. I heard her tell you of my transfer. Well, once we're back East, don't you know how she'll feel? Guilty! She'll regret keeping me from my

40

last trip out with you. If she lives to be a hundred, she'd die feeling guilty."

I couldn't argue with that. You feel that way when you deny something to someone you love. Amanda certainly loved Levi—maybe a little too much. Still, I couldn't shake the feeling that something was going on inside Levi as well, and that it had something to do with what was so troubling to Amanda.

Travis Liston stepped from his office as we passed.

"Any sign of those hard cases who drew down on Sax last night, Travis?" Levi asked.

"No, none. Left town, I guess."

Travis Liston looked just as tough in daylight as he had the night before. My respect for him was rising—not only because he hadn't backed down from me, but because he was a man of few words. He had exhibited that trait the night before when he left without telling me that Levi had put him on to my coming. He remained, even now, a silent statue of a man, his eyes guarded and on me. He was bull of the woods here, and he was pacing his territory cautiously, wondering if maybe another bull had wandered in.

"Morning, Marshal," I said as Levi and I passed on.

Among other things, Liston was reserving judgment on me because he still wasn't sure he had heard the truth behind the shooting in the Cattleman's. Good lawmen have instincts about such things, or they don't last very long. That instinct had him edgy. I was still edgy, too. I couldn't quite put it away as Levi seemed to have done. The only thing that made sense to me was that there had been a bungled attempt at keeping me from reaching Yuma.

The clerk inside the Paxton House called to Levi as we entered. "Mrs. Dupard asked me to tell you she would be in the dining room, Colonel, if you came in before she finished. She wants you to join her there."

A double doorway allowed passage from the lobby into the dining room. We made a right turn and stopped just inside. Levi surveyed the tables. "There she is," he said.

The lady he indicated sat at a table with two men. I gave her the once-over but I couldn't tell much about her from that distance.

"That's Logan and Farley with her," Levi said. "Gives you a chance to gauge those two."

Janna Dupard remained seated as we approached the table, but the two men stood. For some reason or other I found myself hesitant to look at Janna Dupard so I gave my attention over to the men.

Baxter Logan was about Levi's height. Like Levi, his wiry frame looked to possess some strength. He wore a black serge suit, a white shirt, and a black bowtie. That seemed too much clothes for the weather, but Logan appeared not to be suffering any discomfort. His coat was open, and I saw a .44 Colt on his hip. Maybe it was the size of the man, but that gun looked big, seeming to reach from his hip to his knee. The gun looked oiled and well cared for, and he wore it tied down in the fashion of some gunslingers I have known. There was something about him I didn't like. Maybe it was just the gun, but my guard went up at once. I was surprised Levi hadn't mentioned to me the possibility that Logan was a fast gun. He didn't often miss such things.

Logan wore a small mustache across his upper lip that made his mouth look small and tight. That strip of hair was about the size of his eyebrows, and the dark colors of both matched his slicked-down black hair. He had small, dark eyes that seemed to want to bore into me.

Farley was a different type. At first glance, I didn't like him much better, though for different reasons, some of which even I confess were petty. First of all, he was strikingly handsome, the kind of man who knows the right clothes for whatever the occasion and is confident that he has the face and the physique to wear the clothes well. There was on him the stamp of an educated man as well—a Harvard College man perhaps—not that I'd run into many of those in the desert, but I'm a reading man, as I have indicated.

The clothes he wore now looked like they were brand-new, specially bought for the occasion. His brown jacket had broad, deep pockets. I saw the bulge of a small pistol in one. The bottoms of his breeches were tucked into brown boots so polished they glared even in the dull light of the Paxton House cafe.

All that style extended to his face—a broad, handsome face, with brown, clear eyes that managed a twinkle as they took me in. His hair looked freshly cut and manicured. He might have just stepped from his barber's chair, where he had been freshly shaved as well, since his cheeks had that fresh scraped look, and the smell of lotion hung about him.

The only feature about him which didn't seem absolutely perfect was the rich, red tint of his face. Some men get that look from drinking too much, others from business pressure and worry. Of course, Richard Farley might just have a red face, I reasoned.

I put his weight at about two hundred pounds, and there was the look of athletic prowess. Muscular arms extended from the short sleeves of the jumper, and they swung from a pair of shoulders any man might envy. Richard Farley might dress and look like an educated

English dude, but somewhere along the way he had taken the time to develop himself into a physically powerful man.

Farley was nearest to us as we approached the table. He extended a hand to me at once, not waiting to be introduced. "Richard Farley," he said. "You must be Sax Younger."

We shook. The strength in his large hands matched the muscles in his arms. I saw him smile good-naturedly when I tested him.

"And this is Baxter Logan," Levi said.

I would have had to step around Farley to shake with Logan. I was satisfied to accept his nod, which I returned.

"This, my friend," Levi said with something of a flourish, "is Janna Dupard. Appropriate, I think, to save her for last. Wouldn't you agree, Sax? Mrs. Dupard, meet my friend, Sax Younger."

Levi's gallantry was a little overdone. It struck me as false. I wondered if Janna Dupard was a woman who would pick up on that.

I hadn't really looked at her until then. Maybe I'd been afraid to, because I was very, very much aware of her. In fact, the mention of her had brought me from the wild, and she had been on the periphery of my thoughts from that first mention on, her presence shadowing me on the ride south, during the events of the night before, and certainly during the talk with Amanda.

Maybe you're expecting me to say now how beautiful she was. She had beauty—an abundance of it—but hers was a beauty not found in looks or in the shape of her body. It was a beauty that came from inside her, emanating subtly from her pores and from her eyes. I didn't even see that at once, however. You became aware of it as you spent time in her presence.

Not that she didn't have good features. Her eyes were her best. They were large and brown, and the look in them was calm and gentle. There was sadness there as well—a silent and tragic look in their depths. The lashes were long and darker than the thin brows and hair. Those eyes met mine and didn't waver. Amanda had been right. There was grief there.

Her hair was cut short—close to the head, well above her ears, reminiscent of the well-barbered fashion of a man. A flash of gold came from the lobes of delicate ears. And how nice the delicate curve of the neck, made to look longer by the short styling of the hair. High cheekbones managed to diminish the prominence of a nose a little too large for her face. Full lips, slightly parted, showed a line of fine, white teeth.

She had remained seated until Levi introduced us. When she stood, I noted a plain brown riding skirt and scuffed boots. Her blouse was white and resembled a man's white shirt—sleeves were rolled to above her elbows, and the top open a couple of buttons. Her face, arms, and the vee at her neck were sage brown.

I kept looking for something to be on my guard against—some sign of a woman spoiled by position and wealth, someone used to having her way, even some sign she was looking on some rube of the woods, which I certainly was. Not finding any of that, I guess I felt some deflation. I don't know why, unless I was thinking of Amanda, and looking for something that would allow me to refuse, and thus, not lead Levi away from her. On the contrary, everything I saw drew me to Janna Dupard— especially that sadness in the eyes made me want to offer my services, maybe to help wipe it away. Sound romantic? Well, I was feeling that way—a little like a hero in a Walter Scott novel—a veritable Ivanhoe.

"Mr. Younger," she said, offering me her hand, her voice soft, well modulated.

"It's a pleasure," I said. "This comes late, I know, but I'd like to say how sorry I am about your husband and the raid that took your boy. The news about the boy must have given you a lift, however."

As I spoke, my hand engulfed hers, but she made me aware of the strength there.

"We're not absolutely sure Christian is still alive," she said. "It's been almost three years. We won't know, I suppose, until we meet with the Serona."

"But you have good reason to think he is alive," I said. "Else you wouldn't be planning to take on what you must know will be a particularly difficult, demanding trip."

"If I had only the faintest hope he was alive, I'd take no end of difficult journeys," she said. "Thanks to Mr. Logan, there is some hope. He overheard talk of such a raid and of a boy, but not necessarily that he was still alive. But I'll hold on to that, as slim as it may seem, until I know for sure one way or the other."

We had stood until then. She took her seat and nodded for us to do the same.

"Colonel, may I offer you breakfast, and you, Mr. Younger?"

"We've had breakfast. My wife, Amanda, is half in love with Younger. She fed me as she stuffed him. I'll have coffee, though."

"You, Mr. Younger?"

"The same."

A slight smile played about Janna Dupard's lips. I was already a little hot-faced at Levi's remark. That smile made it worse, because obviously she was amused that any woman could be half in love with a clod like me, for that's how I felt—a great, clumsy clod, made to look even more so since I was flanked by Richard Farley.

A waiter, appearing to have overheard, or the recipient of a signal I had not seen, appeared with extra cups and a steaming coffeepot. While he was near, no one spoke.

When he was gone, Janna Dupard said, "Mr. Younger, I feel sure Colonel Piddington has explained why I need your services."

"He has."

"And will you act as my guide?"

"Well, I've ridden that country a time or two scouting the return of Apache before they crossed back over the Rio Grande, but I can't guarantee you a ride that will take you straight to the Serona. May take some time, but I suppose I can say that if they're down there I can find them eventually. That's all I can promise you."

I felt the eyes of Farley and Logan on me, measuring, I suppose, whether or not I was the man they had heard me to be. Most of all, though, I was aware of the disappointed look on Janna Dupard's face.

"I guess I was expecting more," she said.

"In what way?" I asked.

"That you knew exactly where to find the Serona, I suppose. Maybe that you had had some contact with them. Colonel Piddington, and others, told me you knew as much about the Indians out here as any man—probably more."

I think I felt a little afraid that she would suddenly say she had no need of my services if that was the total of my knowledge. Interesting, that I had turned suddenly from being a man hesitant to take my best friend away from his wife into one who now feared he might be dismissed himself. That was quite a turnabout, but it indicates how I had been won over to this woman's cause in a matter of minutes. I had the feeling that maybe I had spoken too honestly if the trip was suddenly so important to me. Maybe I should just clam up. But I couldn't do that. I had to tell her the truth.

"Mrs. Dupard, until Levi told me of the manuscript in your possession, the Serona weren't much more than a legend to me," I said. "I'm sorry to disappoint you. Maybe you'd prefer to find someone else to take you into that country."

She seemed to waver, and I had the feeling she was on the verge of agreeing that such was the case. Until then I still had not been absolutely sure, but suddenly I knew that this trip was as important to me as it seemed to be to Levi. I wouldn't understand the reason for several weeks, but I was sure I had to go.

Suddenly, Farley spoke up.

"That should settle it," he said, sounding almost angry. "We've been told that Younger here is the best guide to be had. Still, he confesses to knowing little of the country and nothing of the Indians. I say the time has come for you to give the whole idea up, Janna. No one feels more for what may have happened to poor Christian than I, but I can't bear to think of the same thing—maybe much worse— happening to you. I beg you, give the whole venture up. Or wait until I'm free to take you myself."

Her jaw tightened. "We've been through this before, Richard," she said. "I have explained to you many times how I feel. I'll say it just once more. I'm determined to go."

But he wouldn't quit. "Wait then," he pleaded. "Wait two months, until I'm free to go. Can I persuade you to do that?"

I'm not master of the subject, but I have to say that what I heard in Farley's voice had the sound of passionate love. I felt better, too, knowing that he hadn't refused completely to go along—would go, if Janna Dupard would only wait. But I must confess that asking her to postpone everything for two months because of business still sounded lame to me.

"No, every day could be crucial," she said.

Still, Farley wouldn't give up. The only explanation was that he loved her so deeply and so feared for her safety he would even risk seriously offending her. I had to admire that, at least. "I don't accept that," he said. "If Christian has lived this long, he'll be alive in two months. I hate to say it, but arriving sooner won't change that. If that sounds too blunt, I'm sorry, Janna. But I feel bluntness is called for."

"Well, I disagree completely, Mr. Farley," Logan said. "I feel sure the boy is alive, that every day counts. Christian is almost nine now. Until now his life with the Serona would have been sheltered."

"Why is that?" I asked, interrupting him.

Logan gave me a glance that seemed to want to sweep my question aside.

"Tell him," Janna Dupard said.

Logan turned back to me. "A boy remains under the supervision of the women much longer among the Serona. When he is turned over to the men, whose purpose is to teach him to hunt and to fight, the dangers increase. I think Mrs. Dupard is right to push on, to get there as soon as possible." He gave me a careful look. "What if you don't know the country down there so well? Everyone out here says you're the best desert guide around. The desert down there is much like the deserts north of the river. I have every confidence you'll lead her safely through to the Serona. Besides, it's my understanding that if you go, Colonel Piddington will be a member of the party."

I found Logan's knowledge interesting. I was familiar with the traditions in many tribes. Not one tribe that I knew waited until their boys were as old as nine to start teaching them to be men. His endorsement of my knowledge and abilities seemed a little too slick as well.

"Where do you get your information?" I asked him.

"From the manuscript left by the priest," he said, managing to show some impatience at my question.

"Apparently, Serona children face great hardships, Mr. Younger," Janna Dupard offered. "The priest, Father Francis Franciscus, writes that the vast majority of the babies die at birth or soon after. That tragic circumstance perpetuates the tradition of keeping those that do survive sheltered longer. The practice of kidnaping to sustain the population of the tribe comes from that as well. Seems terribly cruel, but intellectually I can understand it."

"All that information is a hundred years old," I said. "A lot may have changed since then."

"Why?" Logan asked. "Why would there be a great deal of change when they have lived so isolated all these years?"

I had no answer for that question and didn't attempt to give any. My thought was that change or no, the Serona wouldn't willingly give up a captive they had traveled so far to take.

"Will you agree to guide me, Mr. Younger?" Janna Dupard asked, putting an end to the discussion.

"When do we start?" I asked.

I heard what might have been a sigh of relief from Levi, and just the opposite from Farley. I looked at Logan. The only reaction was in his eyes. Their dark gleam seemed to have increased.

"We'll leave as soon as possible," Janna Dupard said. "I'll leave the business of supplies up to you and Colonel Piddington. Buy whatever you think we will need, and spare no expense. How long do you suppose that will take?"

"A couple of hours if there are some good mustang horses to be had," I said, looking at Levi.

"Anson Palmer just bought some mustang stock," Levi said. "He'll be happy to part with some."

I wanted mustangs who had roamed as near the desert as possible. They would know something of surviving out there. They're used to going longer without water as well, and they know how to locate it. My moros mare was a mustang. She had saved my skin a couple of times.

"We'll leave early in the morning, Mr. Younger, if that'll give you enough time."

"Plenty and more," I said.

"Buy only the supplies you would purchase if only you and Colonel Piddington were to be along. Buy nothing special for me. You understand?"

I wondered how she was going to adapt to hardtack and water with an occasional rabbit and a rattler thrown in. I was glad she said that, though. You don't go into the desert loaded down. A couple of extra canteens, maybe, and a few cans of tomatoes for dehydration.

I rose to go. She stood.

"Don't get yourself killed in some saloon brawl, Mr. Younger," she said. "I'm depending on you."

I turned and looked back. She wasn't smiling. Clearly, she had heard of what had happened the night before. I was reminded of Levi's reaction. I suddenly felt I had to defend myself, which I found strange.

"I don't go around picking gunfights," I said.

"I suppose they seek you out. And do you always manage to finish them as expertly as the one last night?"

"I just try," I said, tired of the game if game it was.

She passed by me. Logan followed close behind. I felt Farley's eyes on me. I turned to face him. He was smiling.

"She don't take to gunfighters," he said. "She can't abide them."

He ran his hand into that big pocket that held his little gun. His eyes were still on me, but his fingers in the pocket seemed to measure the gun's butt. Was he thinking of pulling it out? And did I read a little jealousy beneath the smile? Did Farley not trust her to go into the desert with me? That thought gave me a lift—just the possibility of it. Our eyes remained locked for an instant before he followed Janna Dupard and Logan from the cafe.

"Well, Sax, I'll ride with you out to Palmer's place. We'll pick out the mustangs. How many will we need?" Levi seemed all business.

"Three," I said. "One for you. One for Mrs. Dupard, and a pack mare. I'll ride the moros."

"Only one pack animal?" he asked.

"You heard the lady, Levi. We'll be traveling light."

CHAPTER 6

AMANDA insisted I stay the last night with her and Levi. Remembering that window with no lock, I decided to do that. She and Levi were already at the breakfast table when I came down. Levi, out of uniform and in range clothes, looked a little strange to me. I couldn't recall seeing him dressed like that before. The clothes made Levi seem different—smaller of stature, not so authoritative. Without the uniform he seemed, well, like any other man. I hadn't seen him like that before.

We ate and said our goodbyes to Amanda. "Remember your promise," she whispered at the last moment. "Bring him back safe."

I gave her a reassuring hug, and Levi and I left.

We picked up our mounts at the livery. I looked over the animals I had chosen, and I was still pleased. I had chosen mounts of medium size and weight. The bigger the animal the more it takes to keep him going. Where we were going there wasn't going to be much graze. You want a horse to be lean as well. Too much fat in a horse or a man can be deadly in the desert. Still, you don't want skeletons or midget horses, either. You want endurance and some speed, and these looked to be able to provide both. Yes, I decided I had made good choices. As I looked them over, I checked the bag of grain I had ordered to be hung from the horn of each saddle—emergency food, just in case.

Levi had made his own pick—a lively looking geld, a bay

horse that shaded toward black. The mare I had chosen for Janna Dupard was roan colored with a gentle look to her eyes. She bottomed out well and had legs that suggested she had speed. I gave her a trial run and found that to be true. For the pack animal I chose a clean-limbed mare.

I thought it a trim looking little outfit when I led it to the Paxton House where we were to pick up Janna Dupard. Behind each saddle was tied the sleeping gear of the person who was to ride the horse. Inside each wrap was an extra change of clothes for that person. Levi had called on Janna Dupard for her extras. He had seemed more than willing to do that, which suited me. I hadn't forgotten those last comments she made when we had parted at breakfast.

Both Farley and Logan came out with her. I gave Janna Dupard most of my attention, however. She was sensibly enough dressed—in worn levis and a thick, cotton shirt, whose sleeves she had rolled up. She had on the same scuffed boots, and she wore a hat—a wide-brimmed, flat-crowned hat that would provide some protection. About her waist was a .45, a heavy gun for a woman to carry, and there were the extra cartridges in the belt as well. She seemed unaware of the gun as she came from the hotel, which told me she had worn it before.

The only thing I didn't understand was the medium-sized bag hanging from her shoulder. She saw my eyes on it and said, "Just a few personal items, Mr. Younger. A couple of bottles of lotion for dry skin and some medicines for emergencies." The bag seemed a little bulky for just lotion and medicine, but I had no idea of what else a woman might need, which she might not want to name.

I considered sliding from my saddle and helping her to

mount, but Farley stood nearby and stepped in. He didn't help her up at once, though. Taking her shoulders in his hands, he turned her to face him. Then he lowered his head and planted a kiss on her lips. That kiss seemed like a branding iron, and I watched as a slim brown hand slipped behind his barbered neck and applied some pressure there.

Baxter Logan stood by, his small dark eyes taking everything in. If I hadn't thought so before, that look suggested to me he had more at stake than what appeared on the surface. Had it been Logan who had sent Horse Neck McGraw after me? Both men still stood there before the Paxton House the last time I looked back.

Even with an outfit of only three, a little time is required to shake down to trail ready. Most of that came about on the first day. For instance, there was the question of our positions on the trail. I took the lead. Janna Dupard came next. Levi brought up the rear. Levi had been used to rising at the head of a command, and I wondered if he would eventually chafe in that position.

We made thirty miles the first day, stopping only once at a small spring to give the horses water and a break. The three of us chewed some hardtack and washed it down with water from the spring. The water proved especially sweet, and we emptied our canteens and filled them.

I noted with approval the small amount of water Janna Dupard took in. When you head into the desert, you begin to condition yourself at once to get by on less fluids. Levi knew that, of course, but I had expected to have to explain it to Janna Dupard. That was the first of many instances in which I would be surprised at her knowledge of what she was about on this trip.

We camped that night on the edge of a nice little spring

that was surrounded by a grove of tall cottonwood that hugged that water for sustenance, which goes to show how smart a cottonwood tree can be.

That first camp, we struck a routine that we followed the whole time we were together. Levi saw to the horses, stripping them of their gear and giving each a good rubdown with a handful of grass. He led them to the spring two by two and stood by until he was sure they knew how much water to take in. Of course, with mustangs you don't have to be too concerned about that, but I was happy to see Levi take the care. When each horse had drunk, he staked them on the thickest grass, keeping them as close to camp as possible.

I took charge of the supply pack and laid out the supplies and utensils we would need. I had included very little that was fancy: plenty of dried beans, cornmeal, and flour. There was coffee, of course, and some canned fruit. I have already mentioned tomatoes. I'll explain why they are so important.

Some of us carry too much fat around on our bodies. That fat is dangerous in the desert. The thirst and heat can sizzle it off too fast, leaving a lot of acid poison in the system. Tomatoes help to cut that acid. That's why, after a man has reached a certain stage of dehydration, you feed him tomatoes and tomato juice instead of water. Anyway, that's the way it was explained to me, and I have seen it work. With luck neither of us would reach such a state, but foolish people roam the desert—like they do every other place.

Janna Dupard stood by and watched as I selected what we would need.

"Anything I can do to help?" she asked.

"You know what kind of wood to gather for a fire?"

"The very driest," she answered. "Makes less smoke."

"Lay it beneath that tree there," I said, indicating a smaller, bushy-topped cottonwood. "The leaves and limbs will help to disperse what smoke there is. I'm going to wander out and knock over a rabbit."

I meant that literally. No use wasting a bullet on a rabbit when, if you are careful and quiet, you can get the same results with a rock. I had developed some skill at it over the years. I walked out from the spring about fifty yards and began to circle. I picked up a couple of rocks the right size as I went.

Rabbits settle in under sage, and they stay close to water. I found one soon enough—saw him even before he was ready to hop off. I missed with my first throw, but I brought him down with my second. I took his head off on the spot and skinned him.

Janna Dupard had a nice little fire going when I returned. The rich smell of brewed coffee permeated the camp. She and Levi were enjoying a cup. Levi seemed to be giving her all of his attention as they talked. The thought that Levi had more than a casual interest in Janna Dupard crossed my mind, but I dismissed the idea at once. Levi was happily married to one of the finest women I ever knew, a woman he loved dearly. He was a man who would never look at another woman. Did I completely believe that now, or was I trying to convince myself?

I had cut three limbs and brought them in with me to make my spit with. Two were stouter and had forks at one end. The other was a long slender rod. I set the forks across the fire from each other and ran the slender limb through the hollow of the rabbit. Placing the ends of the slender rod in the forks, I watched the meat begin to roast. The smell of it cooking mingled with the coffee aroma—a pleasant smell about a camp.

A pot of beans sat bubbling on hot ashes that had been raked from the fire. I took a peek and wondered just how hungry Janna Dupard was. There were beans enough in the pot for three meals.

Suddenly, she was beside me, a cup of coffee for me in her hand. She must have read my thoughts.

"I thought I'd cook up a good supply," she said. "We can keep them stored in the pot even in the pack. Won't take much time to heat them up. If we're in a hurry, we can even eat them cold, along with whatever of that rabbit is left. Of course, if it tastes as good as it smells, there won't be any left."

Again I was impressed, and I took a sip of the coffee she handed me.

"Levi said you might return with a rattlesnake," she said. "He says the meat tastes a little like chicken. I was hoping to try some."

"You'll get your chance," I answered. "We'll come across plenty of rattlers out here."

"I expected as much," she said. "I included a snakebite kit in my bag."

There didn't seem anything else to say, and the silence lengthened. I tried to come up with something, but I felt like a clod crouching there on my haunches.

"Colonel Piddington and I have agreed on a first name basis. I'm to call him Levi. He will call me Janna. He says that will be best, since we don't want to advertise he is in the Army. Maybe it would be best if you and I used first names. Shall we agree to that?"

That was a simple thing, but it loomed large in my mind—like she was slipping down a few of the bars between us—the wealth of her family, her obvious education and background, the social position she occupied in St. Louis. I suddenly felt quite good.

"Janna it is then," I said.

"And Sax," she answered.

We made a good supper of beans and roast rabbit which we washed down with coffee. When the meal was finished, I gathered up the dirty utensils and headed for the spring, where I gave them a good scrub with the fine sand around the water's edge.

Levi came in with more wood as I returned. Janna took the stack of utensils and stored them. She had covered the pot of beans and left them near the fire. The remainder of the rabbit had disappeared. I figured it was in the pot with the beans and would reappear at breakfast.

Levi took his bedroll to one side and spread it. His walk was a little stiff now.

"If you two don't mind, I'm going to turn in early. This is one man who needs a long night of rest."

I wasn't sure I liked the sound of that. I went over to where he was removing his boots. Reaching down, I pulled them off for him. I watched as he settled into the bedroll. He did look tired, his face a little pale.

"Are you all right, Levi?" I asked.

He gave me a smile and said, "I know Amanda, bless her soul, asked you to look after me, Sax. But I won't have you checking on my every ache and grunt. Nothing better for a man than to be out in the open like this—good fresh air, and lots of exercise. Makes a man want to lie down and sleep. That's the only thing that ails me. Now you get along."

A wind dipped down. It seemed to have touched the water in the spring, and there was a hint of a chill. Levi pulled his blanket up.

"Should we stand watches?" he asked. "If you think we should, just wake me."

I had given some thought to that and decided there should always be a watch. Looking down at Levi, though, I changed my mind for that first night. I'm a light sleeper, and the moros was as good as a watchdog. Nothing ever slipped up on my camp as long as I rode that mare.

"No need tonight," I said. "We're too close in. I expect we had better take turns once we're over the river, though."

"That'll be tomorrow," Levi said.

"If nothing gets in our way."

"You still worried about something, Sax?" he asked.

"More a feeling than anything else. I keep seeing Logan's face this morning. Hard for me to believe he hasn't some iron in the fire other than the obvious one."

"What's the obvious one?" Levi asked.

"I expect there'll be a reward for all his trouble when this finally comes to an end, whether we bring the boy out or not. The Dupards have all that money. Anything less wouldn't be reasonable."

"You got Baxter Logan on the brain, son," Levi said. "I know he was a Confederate, but other than that I haven't found too much wrong with him. Maybe you stay in the desert too much, Sax. You're turning a shadow into a wolf."

"Maybe," I said, turning away. "You get a good night's sleep."

Janna Dupard wasn't at the fire, but I heard the splash of water from the spring. The sound suggested she was taking advantage of the opportunity for a bath. I decided to do the same when she was finished. In the meantime, I wandered off to a flat, table-like rock that protruded from the ground near the trees. With candles the rock would have looked like a bier. Taking a seat on it, I studied the night sky.

A moon no older than a day or two had come out. It hung in the sky like a thin rind of cheese, the center eaten out. The stars tended to cluster brightest just overhead, which is always the case. They had a friendly look that night—the look I was used to in the desert. Of course, we weren't in what you would call real desert country yet, but we were close enough for me to begin to shed that feeling I got in towns.

I heard a sound behind me and turned. Janna Dupard stood there. In the silver light of that slice of a moon she looked cool and fresh. Her hair clung damply to her head and disclosed even more the delicate curves to her skull. Her face was in shadow except for her eyes. They caught some of the light and cast it back at me.

"May I join you?" she asked.

I wanted her to, but the thought made me nervous. I suddenly had the feeling a moth must have as he circles a flame. Her eyes were the flame, and I had the notion I might be about to go into orbit. There were tricky cross-winds here that I didn't understand and knew nothing about, winds that might sweep me in too close.

"It's a lovely night," she said, not waiting for any comment from me. I had none to make—just that thought.

"Typical of the desert," I responded, "though we're not there yet."

"On a night like this, Sax, I can think of Christian, and I can know he is alive. He will have grown a lot, I know. And he'll have changed. Three years is a long time for a six-year-old to grow, but I'll recognize him. I wonder if he will recognize and remember me? What do you think?"

"A boy never forgets his mother," I said.

"I have had my nights of doubts, but tonight I don't have any. And to think, at long last, I've begun the last leg of the trip to bring him out."

There was a confidence in her voice—more than I had heard before, and I didn't know where it came from. Of course, hope to a mother where her child is concerned is as natural as water to thirst, but this seemed more than just hope.

"Why are you so much surer tonight he's alive?" I asked.

"I don't know. Maybe it's that at last we have started. Maybe it's you—or something about you. It's something I've felt from the moment I saw you."

"It has to be more than that," I said, not sure I wanted to bear the responsibility of such hope.

"Well, tonight my usual feelings seem stronger."

"And what are those?"

"They have mostly to do with Christian—what kind of boy he was. He was an unusual boy. Oh, I know most mothers think that even if they never say it about their children. But Christian actually was."

"In what way?"

"He was a studious little boy even as he was very active. He had a deliberate way about him as well. Even at six he was beginning to think things through. I think those are traits that carry you through difficult situations. I know that expecting Christian to be able to figure out what to do, what it would take to stay alive is, well, optimistic, to say the least. But it's the way I feel."

I had my doubts about her theory. Then I recalled what Logan had said about the Serona delaying the age a boy begins his training for manhood. That might help a boy like Christian to survive. But it still had to be proven the Serona had the boy. I still couldn't see them raiding so far north. I didn't speak those thoughts to her, however. Right then I wanted more than anything to find the boy alive—because it was so important to her.

She changed the subject abruptly. "Levi says you read a lot."

The question surprised me. What right had Levi to . . . "It kills time," I said.

"Seems peculiar—a man of your reputation reading books. What are some of your favorites?"

Her voice had the same quality as when she spoke of the gunfight. I wasn't inclined to let it pass so quickly a second time.

"What talk have you heard of me?" I asked.

"That you have a fast gun. That you've killed a dozen men. Why? Is that not true?"

I thought over what she had said. The figure was hardly an exaggeration—might even be too low. And how do you explain such a thing to a woman from St. Louis, a woman who doesn't understand there are all too many instances when you must kill or be killed. That you have no choice in the matter. About the only thing you can pride yourself on is you kill only those who deserve it, that asked for it.

Did I really believe that? Levi didn't. He had made that clear more than once. How could I expect her to understand?

"I'm not proud of the men I've killed," I said.

"Would you bring them back if you could?"

That was the strangest question of all. Bring back Horse Neck McGraw? Horse Neck was better off dead. If there was a just God, by now Horse Neck was frying in hell. I doubt if anyone would want him back on this earth, including his own mother.

"No, I can't say I would do that."

Seemed to me she was waiting to pounce whichever way I went. Figuring there was no way I could win, I went back to her original question.

"You ask me about books I like to read."

"Yes."

I thought of the copy of Shakespeare and the Bible in my saddlebag. I had almost brought one of them to the rock with me. Would I have the nerve now to take one of them out on this trip? I doubted it.

"I'm fond of many," I said. "Any book can be instructive."

That sounded like the dumbest thing I had ever said. Why hadn't I just named a few?

"Still seems strange. A man who spends his life alone in the mountains and desert. A man who is so feared for his . . ."

She had almost said skill with a gun, but she broke it off.

"Maybe I read to understand why people are the way they are," I said. "Or maybe it's an inherited yearning: my father was a reading man."

"Was?"

"He was killed."

"How?"

Not "I'm sorry," just "how?"

I seldom discuss what happened, but I suddenly wanted her to know it. To tell it to Janna Dupard was appropriate, considering the mission she was on.

"My father, my mother, and I were in a wagon train headed west. It was attacked and overrun by Comanches. They killed the men and most of the women and children. But they spared my mother—took her captive."

"And you? How old were you? How did you escape?"

"I was four. I vaguely remember someone placing Mother and me on a horse that had been hitched to one of the wagons. A Comanche warrior led us away, with my mother holding me before her on the horse. She held me like that for a long time. I remember how tight she held me. When darkness fell, she gave me a long squeeze. Then she lowered me to the ground, holding me by one arm. The horse wasn't going very fast, so I wasn't hurt.

"I guess the Indian didn't miss me. Maybe he was only interested in my mother. Anyway, they never came back. I stayed there on the prairie for several days. I never really knew how many. Must not have been too many, though. I didn't starve. Finally, another wagon train came along. I was picked up by their scout.

"They dropped me off at the next town, a little place called Claybank in Kansas. They thought my mother might be found, that she would look for me in the town nearest where she had dropped me off the horse. She never did, of course."

"She must have loved you very much," Janna Dupard said.

"Why do you say that?" I asked. "She dropped me off in the middle of a prairie."

"And she agonized over it until the day she died. You can depend on that. Only another mother would know how much. Surely, you've been told that before."

"It's what Mrs. Harper used to say."

"Mrs. Harper?"

"The woman who raised me. She was a widow who lived in Claybank. Her husband had been a preacher. She took me in, supposedly until my mother came. I lived with her until I was fourteen. Mr. Harper had been a reading man. I went through most of his books before I went out on my own."

"That's a wonderful, remarkable story, Sax," she said. "It gives me more hope than ever that Christian is still alive."

I had told it for that reason, and I was glad she had found it so.

"I'm going to bed," she said. As she spoke, she laid her small hand on mine. "Thank you for sharing that story with me, and thank you for coming."

She withdrew the hand and went. I watched her back as she walked through the trees toward the dying embers of our fire. Even when I could no longer see her, the warm sensation remained where her hand had touched mine.

But I was more confused than ever. What was her view of me? Was I the charm that insured her son was alive and would be found? Or was I the gunfighter she seemed to have contempt for?

CHAPTER 7

WE crossed the border next day. That night Levi's map showed the first half-inch of the line that would gradually mark our progress into Mexico. The heat increased, but the heavy humidity told us we were still not in the desert. The blistering sun felt like the desert, however. Already Levi and Janna had taken on the looks of seasoned travelers—their faces a deeper tan, their clothes thick with settled dust. I figured I looked the same, except for the increased tan. A couple of days in the sun wasn't going to make much difference in the way I looked. After all, I had lived in the sun for years.

I kept an eye on Levi, but he soon had the kinks worked out, even jokingly pressing me at times to push the horses. I didn't discover any kinks in Janna Dupard. From the beginning she showed a toughness in the saddle that a cowboy would have admired. She never complained of the heat. In fact, as it built she seemed less and less aware of it. I put that down to excitement that the search for Christian was finally underway.

I found my mind on the boy as well. He would have to be a tough youngster to stay alive for three years in a hard land among strangers. I could identify with that some. I had been dropped off that horse into a different world myself. If I hadn't landed in Mrs. Harper's home, there's no telling what would have become of me. But Christian Dupard would have faced tougher odds surviving among the Serona—*if* he had survived, something I found hard to accept. But maybe he had found a substitute mother among the Serona, as I had found in Mrs. Harper.

We made a dry camp that night. Levi's map promised us water just ahead, so we drank freely from our canteens. That was the night Janna Dupard took over the cooking chores. She wasn't asked to do it. In fact, I felt a little strange. I had never turned my cooking fire over to anyone. Levi knew that. He seemed to enjoy the smooth way I was outmaneuvered. I was relegated to the position of observer, except for the meat I provided each night—a rabbit now and then, or a sage hen.

I'll be fair and say the cooking improved. From somewhere, maybe from that mysterious bag she carried, Janna Dupard produced a few herbs and spices that turned even the taste of beans into something to be marveled at. She was fast and efficient as well, never taking more time than I would have required to turn the meal out. It fell my lot to clean up, which I did with as much grace as I could.

I asked her about the spices, but she said, "You have your secrets, Sax. I have mine." But she smiled. I had an idea she would relent if I pressed.

We had begun posting a guard the first night in Mexico. Janna Dupard insisted on taking her turn. We worked her into the rotation, drawing straws that first night to see who would take which watch. I drew the shortest straw and took the first. Janna Dupard followed me. Levi drew the final watch.

I think it was the second or third night I had the long talk with Levi. That conversation gave me some insight into what was happening with him and Amanda. The meal had been served. I had the first watch again. Janna and Levi had settled into their bedrolls. The fire had burned low, but the coals cast up a glow.

I had taken a position a few yards from the fire so the night would open up for me. Staying too close to a fire blinds you at night, turning the darkness into a potential source of danger. I was far enough away not to be troubled by that.

I was out there maybe thirty minutes when I heard someone come up behind me from the fire. I guess I'd hoped it might be Janna Dupard, but I turned and saw Levi.

"Mind if I join you?" he asked, taking a seat on a nearby rock.

The question required no answer. I gave it none.

He didn't say anything for a few moments, but I caught his mood even in the silence. Something had turned him thoughtful. I wondered if thoughts of Amanda had anything to do with it, because I knew Levi couldn't be happy with the way they had parted. Neither was I, and Amanda had been on my mind.

"What is it, Levi?" I asked finally.

Even then he didn't speak—not even to deny that something was troubling him. I had learned long ago that you didn't press Levi into speaking of something before he was ready. Oh, he'd talk, but it wouldn't be about what was on his mind. But apparently he was ready this time.

"You ever think about how fast the years fly by, Sax?" he asked.

Who doesn't by the time they reach thirty—but I could imagine that each year beyond that they picked up speed, and Levi was forty-three.

"Some," I answered.

"I think about it a lot," he said.

"You're only forty-three, Levi. That's a long way from old age."

"Not so long," he answered.

He sounded like a man who needed to get something off his chest.

"What's botherng you, Levi?" I asked, my voice suggesting I was more than willing to listen, or at least I hoped it did.

"Well, a lot of things, Sax. You begin to think about a lot of things."

"Such as?"

"You think about all the things you promised yourself you would do when you were growing up. You measure what you've done against those dreams. When there is a lot of difference, you begin to feel you failed."

"Well, that can't be your problem, Levi. Look at what you've done."

"What?" he asked.

His voice sounded contemptuous. That surprised me. I had always thought Levi took a lot of pride in what he had done.

"Well, for starters, you helped put the best fighting Indians in the West onto a reservation. No Army man was more respected by the Apaches. You've helped bring law into a wild territory. That's nothing to sneeze at. And you've had a happy life with the woman you love—and what's more important, a woman who loves you."

"I can't deny that," he said.

"Well then?"

He was silent for a moment. A coal from the dying bed behind us snapped suddenly. A cricket chirruped in the grass nearby. In the distance a wolf pack announced their hunt. I waited for Levi to speak.

"It isn't enough, Sax," he said.

"Seems like a lot to me, Levi. Amanda mentioned the transfer back East. Is that it?"

"Maybe. They'll put me behind a desk, which'll mean the end of my career—no more promotions. Eventually, I'll be pensioned off. Amanda and I will squeeze pennies for the rest of our lives, just to make ends meet."

There was more bitterness in his voice now. But I understood more fully why this trip into the desert to search for the boy, even the possible contact with a hostile tribe was important to him. The trip meant more than just a last fling in the wild with me as well. In Levi's mind, it was a last hurrah. He saw it as a fond goodbye to a life he had loved—maybe a way to leave it without such a feeling of failure.

"Does it also have something to do with having no children, Levi?" I asked.

"I . . . I don't know, Sax," he said. "I always wanted kids. Amanda did, too. When we didn't have any, it was a major disappointment to both of us. Maybe I would feel different if I had a son and could see him begin to take up a life. I suppose any man feels more successful when he can look at his children and see his life continue on in them."

I didn't know what to say to that. The blow had been a cruel one, of course. But others had faced it. I had faith Levi would.

"Not that it's any consolation, Levi, but you've been something of a father to me."

"No," he said, "it's been the other way around." He reached out and put a hand on my shoulder. "Amanda and I have spoken of it many times. She loves you like a son. Of course, that's obvious the way she fusses over you."

"Yes," I said.

"Do you remember the first time we met, Sax?" he asked.

He began to chuckle. Already the depression which had burdened him seemed to have lifted. Maybe talking had helped, or maybe the memory of our first run-in was what lifted his mood.

"I have an idea you're going to remind me," I said, my own mood lifting a little with his.

"You came charging down that valley with fifteen Apaches on your tail. Your horse was wearing down, and the Apaches knew it. They already had your scalp swinging at their waists. You came up to a fair-sized patch of rock, enough to make a stand in. You flung yourself from your mount, rifle in hand, and plunged behind a boulder. I never saw a man pump a rifle faster." He topped for a moment. "Never saw better shooting, either. You took out six of the warriors before they made it to the rocks."

"And you let them get there," I said. "You and a dozen troopers sitting out there among rocks yourself, waiting in ambush for the same bunch that were chasing me, and you let them nearly get to my hair before you took a stand."

"Well, I did wait a mite long," he said. "I wanted to see how many you could take out by yourself. Of course, I recall you didn't appreciate our taking a hand even then. When the shooting had stopped, and the dust settled, you came out of the rocks as mad as a wet setting hen. You insisted you could have taken the whole bunch if we had only held our fire. Told me that several times—then and later."

"I was a fool kid, Levi. At seventeen, we don't show much sense."

"I practically had to arrest you to take you in with me. Had more trouble after that talking the colonel into hiring you on as a scout. He vowed no seventeen-year-old kid could track and reconnoiter the way I claimed you could. I made a bet with him. You remember the mount I owned then?"

"A blood bay gelding," I said.

"That's the one. Lambert had had his eyes on that horse for some time. I bet him the horse you were as good a scout as he had in the outfit. You remember? He rode out with us on the next patrol."

"I remember, but you never told me this before. Why?"

"I . . . I don't know, Sax. Just never seemed important," he said.

"What if I had failed? After all, you didn't know all that much about me."

"I knew enough."

"What?"

"Well, I'd heard the tales of this towheaded kid who roamed Kansas and half of Texas looking for the Comanches who had made off with his mother. Any man who could do that, seventeen or no, and stay out of the hands of the Comanches, or Comancheros, for that matter, was better than any scout in Lambert's command."

"So you won the bet," I said.

"More than just a bet," he said.

I didn't ask him what. I knew.

We sat there for a few moments longer. Behind us the fire was completely out. I heard the wolves again. They sounded different somehow. I suspected they had made their kill.

Levi stood up. "Thanks," he said, dropping his hand to my shoulder once again.

He went back to his bedroll. I sat there and watched the night and waited for the time when I would wake Janna Dupard up. I thought of Levi. He had unloaded to me, and I thought it had helped. And, as any friend will, I took part of his burden on myself. Of course, I didn't mind, not after what Levi had been to me since that day he rescued me from the Apaches.

CHAPTER 8

THE next few days and nights passed uneventfully. Levi added another inch or so to his line on the map, sighting by the stars at night with his instruments. He seemed to have put thoughts of failure from his mind. At least, he didn't speak of it to me again.

I wondered if the search for Christian Dupard was responsbile for some of his thoughts. That he felt deeply for Janna Dupard was obvious. Had the search, and Janna Dupard's silent grief, brought Levi's own desire for children to the fore again? Of course, there was no way I could answer that question without discussing it with Levi, and I wasn't inclined to do that.

But I couldn't shake from my own mind how the boy had become something of a focus inside me as well. For instance, I had not, for many years, dredged up the way I felt that night when I was dropped from the horse into the darkness of the prairie. My God, how frightened I was! But I hadn't cried. I had been too much afraid to do that. I didn't want the Indians to hear me and come back. I wanted my mother, though. God, how I had wanted her. Somehow I knew she wouldn't return for me. That the Indian who had led the horse wouldn't let her. I hadn't recalled those feelings for years. Why now, if not for the boy? And I found myself thinking of my mother again, wondering what had become of her. Had she been treated well by the Comanche warrior?

I was relieved about one thing, however. As we worked

our way deeper and deeper into the Mexican desert, I became convinced that my suspicions of Logan were groundless, that my run-in with Horse Neck, Skittles, and Lawson was what it appeared on the surface to be—a foiled attempt at murder and robbery, followed by a long ride for revenge for being left afoot in the wild. Any man might have followed up on that. Without a horse out there you don't stand much of a chance. Of course, that trio hardly deserved horses.

We were deep in the desert now. The closed-in feeling which had made me uneasy in Yuma was a thing of the past. There was space here—wide open space, as far as you could see in every direction and straight up as well. The air was hot as hell, but it was pure, no sorting out the smells you pick up in a town, just clean, clean air. And silence. Except for the creak of your own leather, the stamp of your horse, or your own breathing. The other sounds, the sounds of the wild, you registered as part of the silence.

From time to time, I spotted dust trailing up—whether from deer, wild horses, or mounted men, there was no way of telling. I always pulled up, though, putting a stop to our own dust until the other trailed away. Once or twice I caught glimpses of riders, or I thought they were riders. The way the distance shimmers in the desert it's sometimes hard to tell.

I was allowed a spell at the cooking fire one night. I had killed a rattler, skinned him, and brought him in. Janna stepped aside and allowed me to cook him. She professed to like the meat, and she cooked the next one, adding a few of those ingredients, which I confess outdid my own efforts.

The increasing heat became a thing we fought from

sunup until sundown. I stood it well enough, but Levi and Janna suffered. I fed them tomatoes, making them drink juice as well. On the hottest days the sun was dazzlingly brilliant, beating down relentlessly, heating saddle leather and metal into something that burned the flesh. Often the wind blew out of the southwest like hot breath on your face. Constant, always pressing, it never seemed to vary—like a tooth that aches dully hour after hour.

On other days there was a stillness on the land. There was no wind, nothing that seemed alive, but the three of us and the horses. On such days the shimmering horizon allows the eyes to conjure up strange visions—cool, enticing bodies of water, floating just off the ground, looking very real. Like a lot of things in life, however, they stay just beyond your grasp.

I began to select our campsites with more care. When we found water, we no longer camped beside it. Supplying our needs, we camped some distance away amid some cover. Waterholes in the desert are like the busiest corners in a town. Travelers within fifty miles converge on them—Indians, outlaws, renegades—take your choice—we weren't anxious to meet up with any.

I also chose our camps with an eye to defense—a cave in a canyon wall, in the center of a few boulders, or among a few trees when there were trees, which was very seldom. If strangers did stumble upon us in the darkness, we would have a chance to fight them off, and that did happen one night.

Janna had the watch. She shook me awake.

"Sax, I think there is something out there."

We were camped against a cliff. I sat up, grabbed my rifle, and headed for the front of the camp. I remember being thankful for that cliff. It leaned out over our camp and gave us protection from above and from one side. I was still not sure Janna hadn't heard an animal on the prowl.

But I had told her to take no chances, that she was to wake me at any sound or movement she couldn't explain. I had also taught her the sounds the moros made when another horse came close in.

We dropped down behind a boulder that fronted the camp. I surveyed the dark scene—a rock-studded valley a mile or so across with a small ooze of water near one end, a water hole we had visited. There was no moon, and I couldn't see much. Only the pale light from the stars diluted the darkness. The mare was restless, however.

"What did you hear?" I asked in a whisper.

She didn't answer right away. "I . . . I didn't exactly hear anything," she responded. "I just had this feeling. That sounds foolish, I know, but it was very strong. I felt I was being watched or something. I feel a little silly now, getting you up like this."

"No, you did right."

I wasn't one to deny that such a thing can happen. When you live alone in the wild, certain senses you can't put a name to develop again. Animals who survive have it. Man once lived that way: He had it as well, but it withered away as it no longer was needed. It remains stronger in some than in others.

I crouched there in the dark, my eyes and ears tuned to the valley. Suddenly, some distance out I saw a shadow flit from behind a rock, dash across an open space, and drop behind another rock. I saw another. Then another.

"Wake up Levi," I whispered. "Be very quiet. I don't want them to know we're onto them."

"You mean there is someone out there?"

"I've counted three."

"Three?"

"There may be more."

She scrambled away to wake Levi, and I searched the darkness for more than the three. I didn't see any more, however.

Levi dropped down beside me, his rifle in his hand. Janna came to the other side. She had her rifle also, and the big Colt hung in its holster. Levi began to study the valley. I gave him a moment, not pointing out the darting shadows.

"Three," he said then. "Is that all?"

"Maybe they left a guard on their horses—wherever their horses are," I said.

"Probably back at the water hole," Levi added. "They must have picked up our sign there about dark."

"They've got good eyes," I said. "I rubbed that sign out."

"Well, they saw something. They didn't just sense we were here."

I didn't say anything, but that's what Janna had done. Maybe the moros gave her a little help.

"Well, how do we handle this, Sax?" Levi asked.

"You're the military man. You tell me."

He thought about it for a moment. "Go back to the bedrolls," he said then. "Make them look like we're in them. I'll keep an eye on these prowling coyotes while you do that."

"What then?" I asked.

"We'll settle in against that cliff. We'll let them come in. When they're ready to slip a knife into us, we'll load them up with lead."

"Sounds about right to me," I said.

"You mean kill them in cold blood?" Janna asked.

Her voice reflected the disapproval I had heard in it before—mainly when the subject of my reputation with a gun came up.

"It's what they plan to do to us," I said.

"Still, there is a difference. We're not outlaws."

"But they are," Levi said. "Give them the chance and they'll kill their own mothers for a horse."

"But we don't know all that," she said.

"We can't risk taking them alive," I said. "One might escape and spread the word we're out here. That would bring a whole pack down on us."

I didn't mention the fact that if word spread there was a woman in the party even more would come.

She didn't argue further, but I knew she wasn't reconciled to the trap we were about to spring. She followed me back to the bedrolls and helped me make them look occupied. When that was finished, I took her hand and faded back along the cliff, looking for a place for us to lie in wait. I found just the spot.

"You wait here," I said. "I'll get Levi."

I moved silently back through the camp. Levi was still crouched behind the boulder.

"Where are they now?" I asked.

"There," he said, pointing to rocks maybe fifty yards out.

"Did you spot any more?"

"No, just the three."

"The bedrolls are fixed. I left Janna along the cliff. Let's get back there and wait for them."

He fell in behind me. Janna still seemed troubled when we joined her. I looked for signs of fear, but I didn't see any. Not that I had expected to. We settled in to wait.

But not for long. A moment later I saw the silhouette of

a man rise up from behind the boulder we had just left. He studied the camp for a moment. The bedrolls were in plain view. Obviously, he saw them and salivated with greed. Three defenseless men who waited to be robbed— who waited for his knife. He gave a signal. The other two came up behind him. He pointed to the bedrolls. We watched as he pointed out which bed each would take.

"I'll give the signal," Levi said in a soft whisper.

I felt Janna stiffen.

They moved in on the beds as silently as a puma stalking prey. Watching them, knowing they were there, I still didn't pick up a sound. That's how good they were. Then the thought hit me. What if they were Serona? What better way to gain entrance into the Serona village than with captives.

Levi was within a yard of me. I reached a hand out to his arm and leaned close to his ear. "We'll take them alive," I barely whispered. "They might be Serona."

That was enough for him to understand.

By then the three were poised above the bedrolls ready to strike.

"There are a half-dozen rifles with itchy trigger fingers aimed at you," Levi said in Spanish. "You make a move, we'll pump you full of lead."

I could feel their panic. It was my first inkling they weren't Serona. No Indian would have reacted that way.

"Don't shoot," one of them said in a Texas drawl as thick as molasses.

"Drop the knives then," Levi ordered.

Three knives made a clatter against the stone floor.

Levi stepped from the shadows. I put a hand out to Janna and indicated she was to remain hidden. Then I followed Levi.

"Stir up the fire, Sax" Levi said. "Let's see the faces of the curly wolves we've captured."

"Stand together to the side there," I said. "Keep them covered, men. Shoot if you see one move."

I was carrying the bluff Levi had begun a little further. The three would soon know it was a bluff, but with some light maybe we could have them disarmed before they knew.

I stirred the warm ash which had been our fire. A few red coals remained at the bottom. I piled dry shavings on those and watched them sprout a flame. I piled mesquite limbs on that, stepped back, and waited. A few moments later their faces were lit.

They were white men—renegades if I read their appearances right. One was a very large man with red hair and beard. That he was the leader was clear. He had pushed his hat to the back of his head. It hung there by a string which was around his neck—a tall Texas hat to match the accent I had heard. With the first wavering flame, he began to study the rocks for the extra guns. I got ready.

A second man was Mexican. He wore a wide sombrero that flopped a little to hide his features. Dusty black hair fell from beneath the hat to his shoulders. The third was a blond, pimply faced kid. I saw a crazy glint in his eyes as the fire built.

All three wore filled holsters.

"Unbuckle your guns," Levi ordered.

Redhead gave a grunt. The three seemed to work at holster buckles, but they took their time.

It happened quickly then. Redhead gave a second grunt, and they went into action. That signal, too subtle to catch, and the quick response of the others, suggested they had been together a long time.

I dropped my rifle and made a downward grab for the old Colt, a better weapon for close-in fighting. I figured at least two of those guns would be aimed at me, and I threw myself to the side as I brought the old gun out. Redhead was the most dangerous. I concentrated on him, shooting for the body, as you should in a gunfight if you've got any sense. He took my first bullet in his chest. He was spun around, going down with another grunt, this time a much louder one.

I rolled and came up looking for the other two. Meanwhile, guns had been popping all around me. I was too late to help with the Mexican and the kid. They were stretched out beside the fire. Levi, with his six-gun curling a wisp of smoke, stood a few steps back from them.

"Didn't put up much of a fight, did they?" he said.

I turned to Janna Dupard. She had come out from the cliff. I never saw a face so pale. She held the big Colt in her hand, but she hadn't used it. I didn't have to check the gun to know that. The look on her face was enough—that and the way she held the gun down beside her. Stepping to her side, I eased the gun from her hand.

She let me as she stared at the dead men. Then she looked up at me. For a moment I thought she didn't know me. Her eyes were on me, but her mind was someplace else, maybe still in that moment of exploding guns and death.

Then she seemed to mentally shake herself. She said, "I . . . I'm sorry. It all happened so fast. I didn't even help."

"That's the way it always is," I said. "No time to second-guess or think."

"And that's the way it was with all those . . . others?" she asked.

I knew what she meant, and mostly it was true. But any

man, unless he's a better man than I ever was, knows it isn't like that every time. That in each of us there is apt to be lit a spark that loves the challenge of that moment—to see who is best, who is swiftest, who will be crowned king of the walk—the fastest gun.

But I said, "Yes, it was mostly like that." I didn't look at Levi.

Levi and I dragged the bodies from our camp. We didn't go through their pockets looking for a name. There would have been no use, though somewhere a mother, a sweetheart, maybe a wife, might sadly wait for word, and wonder if it would ever come. Of course, it wouldn't. The three were now among the thousands the West had silently swallowed up.

Janna made coffee. We drank it as the fire died out again. Still, we lingered as the coals turned from red to gray. I watched the red light play across Janna Dupard's face and then die out. I don't think I was ever so unable to read my feelings about another person. But somehow my own roughness didn't seem to matter so much anymore. Had she made me feel that way, or was I deluding myself?

I took over the watch and ordered Janna and Levi into their bedrolls. I doubt they slept much, though.

I watched dawn creep into that rock-strewn valley, glad daylight had come, though I knew it would bring the heat. I rebuilt the fire and heated the coffee which was already made. Janna Dupard rose from her bed and began our breakfast. Levi seemed slow to rise.

"I've misjudged you," Janna Dupard said, giving me a look from over the fire. "I want you to say you forgive me."

I never felt so squeezed in my life. One word would lower the barriers between us. All I had to do was say yes. I was tempted—sorely, sorely tempted, but I held it back.

"There are things inside me you don't know about," I finally said. "Things I don't want you to know about."

She gave me a look that said she doubted that, and she went back to whipping up our food. Levi rolled out then. We saddled our mounts as she cooked. When we had eaten we rode out. I felt nothing but relief, but relief from what I didn't figure out for a long time.

CHAPTER 9

MY judgment of our mounts proved out. Even when there was no grass they nibbled away at sage and other trash graze. That and a handful of grain each day held them until we reached a water hole that had some grass. The moros, along with the others, led us to water more than once after they caught a faint whiff of dampness on the desert air. Sometimes there was no more than a panful. Often that was steaming hot. But we would shade it and split it first among the horses, and then wait for more to collect for us.

A couple of times we found small islands of green in the desert, a few trees, even a bird or two. And there was plenty of graze for the mustangs. We risked staying over a few hours at those to let the horses fill their bellies and stock up on the water. We took turns standing guard and soaking up moisture ourselves, Levi and I lying flat in the water in nothing but our underwear. Janna took her turn. I don't know what she lay flat in.

I didn't forget the Serona. I still chose campsites that could be defended whenever that was possible. And we kept vigilant watches. The desert at night, even with no moon, is surprisingly bright. The sand and rocks give off their own light. Anything that moves is easily spotted. And when there is no wind, the sound carries far; even the soft crunch of a boot on sand cannot be disguised.

When the wind did blow, the whipping sand and dust blotted out everything. When there was a serious blow, which happened a couple of times, we sat huddled beneath blankets, our backs to a boulder away from the wind, and waited it out. Sandstorms come up fast and are gone just as quickly. We were thankful for that.

Actually, I was more concerned during daylight hours. There was no way to hide our dust. Often when we left the sand, we traveled through terrain made to order for ambush . . . steep, varicolored cliffs and peaks split by narrow, winding canyons. I tried to search out every niche, and I depended on the moros.

Levi stayed alert as well. He was a man who had set a few ambushes of this own, avoiding a few as well. He spotted the dust that was to dog our trail first. We stopped and waited until it passed on, hoping we hadn't been seen. Each time it reappeared, sometimes closer in, sometimes further back, as though they were playing with us. That went on for a couple of days, making us feel safer when night shut the desert down.

We began rising earlier, getting underway before our dust could be seen. That helped some. When daylight came, the dust seemed farther away. Of course, it was always there, as constant as the sun. I thought of traveling only at night and getting our rest during the day. But I didn't suggest it. There would be no sleep in the heat, and we would soon wear ourselves down.

We speculated on who was out there. The most obvious guess was the Serona. I began to hope it was. After all, we had to make contact with them sometime. Why not now? Of course, I was nervous about making contact. I had no idea how we would be received—especially when they learned our mission. But the priest had lived among them. Logan had hired them. They had to know there were white men who were peaceful.

But I rediscovered my old suspicions of Logan. There were other possibilities as well. More bandits. Maybe even Mexican soldiers had got wind of our presence in the desert.

Then came the day that tail of rising dust began to close in on us.

"What should we do, Sax?" Levi asked. "Make a run for it?"

I was tempted, but there was the possibility we would be running away from the very ones we needed to make contact with.

"I think we'll hole up and wait for them," I said.

"You think they are Serona then?" Janna asked.

"Well, we'll know when they catch up with us," Levi said.

We were traveling through medium rough terrian—undulating ridges and coulees with deep sand in between. A mile or so ahead I spotted a ridge whose summit had something of a mesa look to it. There was cover as well. Rocks waist-high or higher. The slope up was clear except for an occasional boulder half-buried in sand. If we had to fight, we would be firing down, and we would have a clear field of fire. You can't ask for much more advantage.

"There," I said, pointing to the slope. "We'll wait for them up there."

There was no need to push the horses. The dust was still a few miles back. As we rode, I turned to offer some assurance to Janna. I still remembered the look on her face after the other shootout. She looked more determined now, and she had taken the big six-gun out to check its load.

That ridge top wasn't a bad place to make a stand. The bit of flat tabletop had plenty of cover. The sand on the slope reached the knees of the horses at times. There would be no fast charges. If they rushed us, we could make them pay a price.

But how long could we hold out if they didn't rush us? Food was no problem. Water was. Our canteens were low, and we had to think of the horses. We could hold out maybe a couple of days, I decided. After that, well . . .

I counted twelve as they swept into the valley. Spotting us at once, they formed a line beneath us, stretching out along the valley floor. Most were dressed in the white cotton suits of the Mexican peasants, and they wore the familiar wide, heavy hats. They could have been Serona, except for one. He was dressed differently—a lot more fancy. He wore a dark suit and knee-length boots. I caught the gleam of silver conchos down his legs—colorful dress for the desert. The band of his sombrero gleamed as well. More silver. The gear on his horse flashed in the sun.

They were well-armed. Each brandished a new-looking rifle. About their shoulders hung bandoleers of extra cartridges. They made a formidable line along the valley.

"What are they doing holding back?" Levi asked, pointing toward two riders who had held up in the mouth of the valley.

"Beats me," I said. "But the ones we have to worry about are those down there."

Fancy dresser sent his horse, a fine black stallion, a few paces up the slope. I could see him better now. He was heavyset, with a black mustache that curled out from his face and up against heavy jowls. He sat there a moment. I could see the sweat on his swarthy face. He made a move to come even closer.

"That's far enough," I said, showing him my Winchester. "State your business from there."

"Señor Younger? It is Señor Younger, no?"

His accent was heavy Spanish, a fact that registered only barely with me, as I got over the surprise that he would know my name.

"I'm Younger," I said. "But how did you know? What do you want with me?"

"Ah," he laughed. "We know many things in the desert, Señor Younger. Sometimes we find things out in strange ways. Sometimes not so strange. As to how I came to know who you are—that isn't important. As for what we want: nothing more than the money the lady carries in her bag."

I laughed. "You're barking up the wrong tree," I said. "None of us are carrying enough money to split between twelve men, and that's not counting the two back there who seem a little shy."

He returned my laugh. "You don't know then?" he asked.

"Know what?"

"The contents of the bag. Or is it you are a good bluffer, Señor Younger. You play poker, yes?"

I felt a little less like laughing as I recalled the size of that bag and how it never seemed to be very far from Janna Dupard. Still, I couldn't believe she could have brought very much money along, not without telling me. I looked at her. One look was all I needed.

"How much?" I asked.

"Fifteen thousand."

I might have taken a punch to the belly and felt better. I turned to Levi.

"Did you know?"

"No," he said. "I had no idea."

"We just want the money, Señor Younger," the big Mexican shouted. "Give it to us. Toss the bag down. You and the lady and your colonel friend can ride out then.

You can ride on to search for the Serona, or head back for the border, whichever you prefer."

My head was spinning a little. That was enough money to attract every outlaw and renegade on both sides of the border if word leaked out, as it had, apparently. Janna stirred nervously beside me.

"Why?" I asked.

"I thought I might have to pay a ransom."

"But why didn't you tell me?"

"I was told you wouldn't let me bring it."

"Who told you that?"

"Logan. Farley agreed."

"That son of a bitch," Levi said.

"Who? What?" Janna Dupard asked, a little flustered at Levi's language.

"He means Logan," I said. "It was an elaborate setup—just a way to get you out here with the money. The only question I have is, why did they wait so long?"

She gave a laugh—a very unnatural sort of laugh. She had control, but she was struggling. She was thinking that if money was behind the scheme, Logan's story about her boy was nothing more than bait. That sank in, and I could see how much she was hurting behind the mask she made of her face. She was living again through the death of the boy.

I hurt, too, for the boy . . . and for her. But anger crept through me like thick syrup. I fought it, for an angry man makes mistakes of judgment. I couldn't afford mistakes if we were to survive.

I turned to study the distant men. "Could one of them be Logan?" I asked.

"Maybe the smaller one. He's the right size," Levi said.

I looked at the larger man. They were a long way from

us, but something about him looked familiar as well. Farley? No, it couldn't be. Richard Farley was in love with Janna. He was Yancey Dupard's best friend. There was no way he could be a part of this.

"Señor Younger!" the man below us called. "You have had time to think now. Throw down the money."

"Give it to them!" Janna said.

"No, we can't do that," I told her.

"Why not?" she asked. "I don't care about the money."

"I know, but I hope you care about our lives."

"What does that mean?" she wanted to know.

"It means they can't afford to let us get out of here alive. We'll keep the money until we figure something out."

"Let them rush us," Levi said. "We can pick them off as they charge up that slope."

"They won't charge before dark, Levi."

"What'll we do then, Sax?"

"We'll play for time. Wait for dark. Maybe we can slip away before they attack."

"Señor Younger, the day grows late! Throw the money down!"

"We may decide to give it to you!" I called, "but not just now."

There was a pause filled with frustration. "When then?"

"Who are you?" I called. "What's your name?"

I didn't know if he would play that game, but I expected he was a show-off. His clothes said that much about him. A lot of outlaws have that weakness. Not as many would get hanged if they could keep from bragging about their misdeeds. I doubted this one was any different. Anyway, the more we knew of him and the two men out there, the better—though how we would use it, I still had no idea.

"My name isn't important," he called.

"Well, somebody did a hell of a job tracking us like this. I'm good myself, but someone in your bunch is better. But I don't suppose it was you."

"My name is Geraldo Bustamente!" he said with hardly a pause. "Now will you throw the money down?"

"Who are the two men out there?" I asked, indicating the two who still hung back.

"They are nobody important," he said. "Just two ignorant peasants who wish to join my little army. I have let them ride along so I can look them over. They hold back because they are not trained."

"Mr. Bustamente!" I called. "I can tell you aren't a very smart man, but what do you take us for?"

"You insult me?" he blustered.

"I think those men are your bosses. You tell them I will discuss turning the money over only with them."

"I speak for them, Señor. To have them ride here would serve no purpose. Maybe you don't want to know who they are, you understand me? What one doesn't know one can't ride away with, eh? Is that not so, Señor?"

"You could be right," I said. "I tell you what, you ride over and speak with them. See if they wish to remain unknown."

I could almost hear his frustration. He turned and looked at his men, and then back up at us.

"Or would you rather order a charge in broad daylight," I added. "I hate to think of the blood of that fine stallion turning the sand into red jelly. Think of the pity, Señor Bustamente."

He sat there another moment. Then he said, "I will tell them." Turning the black about, he rode toward the men at the mouth of the valley.

"You don't think they'll ride in for a talk, do you?" Levi asked.

"I doubt it, but maybe you should keep a watch on the slope to our backs. They might have more men back there."

Levi moved across the narrow mesa top and knelt behind a rock, studying the next valley. "You were right," he called. "I count five. Looks like they've got us boxed."

Seventeen, a number that sounded plenty more dangerous than a dozen, for some reason or other. Levi stayed there to keep an eye on the back slope. I watched Bustamente ride down the valley.

He reached the two. They talked for a time. Then Bustamente started back. He kept to the middle of the valley now, collecting his men as he reached them. They fell in behind him, and he led them across the valley. They dismounted, some dropping into the sand to rest. Others began to gather the dead mesquite.

"They're going to cook," Janna said—surprised, I suppose, that they would think of food.

I was happy to see it. I had bought some time. Now I had to come up with a plan.

"Eating is not such a bad idea," I said, hoping she would take the hint. Cooking might get her mind off the boy for a while.

"There is no firewood up here," she said.

"Over here," Levi called. "There is mesquite over here."

"Won't take much of a fire to heat some beans," I said, tossing her my knife to hack the wood.

She worked quickly about the little fire she made. I think it helped, but only a little. She couldn't free herself of the idea that the boy might not be alive, that Logan had played an elaborate con on her. That was my first thought as well, but the more I mulled it over, the less certain I became. The scheme was too elaborate. There was the manuscript, and Janna had had Logan checked out. He had hired Serona to work on his ranch. Maybe the word he brought of the boy was true. What could be more convincing as bait than the truth? Maybe he had heard the story, checked it out, and then came up with the scheme for the money.

"Who suggested you pack along that ransom money?" I asked her.

"Logan," she said.

CHAPTER 10

WE could do nothing but wait, hoping that when darkness came we could slip through that line of men facing us from either side of the ridge, and hoping, too, that we could do that before they made their move on us.

Janna served some tomatoes and canned fruit with her meal. I explained how tomatoes work on the body when the desert heat has sucked it dry of fluids. The fruit was a little like dessert. We hadn't had much that was sweet since leaving Yuma, but you shouldn't take in too much sweet in the desert, anyway. We dawdled over it, all three of us, prolonging the eating of it in order to have something to do, rather than just sit and watch the men below.

The sun finished working its way down the sky. As its edge rested on the rim of the western horizon, a purple flush crept up the sky from the east, and then grew darker, as the sun, resembling a large, overripe orange, poised itself to slip behind a distant, low line of hills. The first hint of a chill pervaded the air, and below us the men of Geraldo Bustamente began to build up their fires.

"They don't seem worried about the Serona, building up those fires like that," Levi said from his position across from us. "I guess we still have a ways to go before we can expect to make contact with them ourselves."

I agreed, but I didn't find it necessary to answer.

Darkness came steadily on. Still I caught Janna's gaze on me. Maybe I felt it as much as I saw it. That's how much she was in my mind.

"Is something wrong?" I asked.

"I have a suggestion to make," she said.

"What?"

"If we do get through, we should head straight for the Rio Grande. This has gone far enough. I was foolish to hope that after three years the word about Christian was true. I should have listened to Richard."

I knew how much saying that cost her. She was snuffing out any renewed hope that the boy was still alive, a hope she had held onto for months now. That's a terrible thing for a mother—to have a child restored to her who has been lost, even if only in her mind, and then to have him snatched away again.

"Are you saying you want to give up the search?" I asked. Give up any more effort to make contact with the Serona?"

"It's best. Before I get us all killed out here. Of course, it may be too late. We may never get off this ridge."

I didn't answer for a moment. I didn't want to get her hopes up all over again, but I had actually begun to believe there could be something to Logan's story. There was something else I wasn't completely sure of as well. We had only our suspicions that one of the men out there was Logan. The evidence seemed strong, but it was only circumstantial.

"Maybe it's possible Geraldo Bustamente came by his information some other way. If there was a chance of that would you still want to give up?"

The valley below had become shrouded in darkness. Even on the ridge the light was waning fast. I could see Janna only dimly, but I saw the quick uplift of her head.

"How else could he have learned about it? No one else knew."

"Did you pick up the money in Yuma?"

"Yes, I had it transferred from St. Louis. It was waiting for me when I arrived."

"You drew it out of the bank then?"

"Yes."

"Well, fifteen thousand is a lot of money. Someone from the bank—a clerk, one of the higher-ups, even another customer, might have mentioned it to someone outside the bank. You, Farley, or Logan might have spoken of the money in the hotel lobby or in the cafe. The point is, word of it might have spread that way. In that case, Logan might not be out there. But even if he is, I've had another thought."

"What?" she asked.

"Why did you believe his story in the first place?"

"There was so much to back it up. The manuscript. He checked out. I believed it because . . ."

"That's my point—the way I've begun to think. There might be something to the story Logan brought you. Maybe we should think along those lines until we know for sure."

"How will we ever learn the truth?" she asked.

"Well, if we are correct, and that's Logan out there, we might get a chance. I don't think we should run for home until we explore that possibility."

"If I could only talk to him!" she said. "I could read the truth in his eyes! And if you think there is any possibility of that, we mustn't give up. We will go on—that is, if I can persuade you and Levi to do that."

"I signed on for the duration," Levi said.

"So did I," I said after him.

Whether it was the right or wrong thing, I had stirred her up again. That took very little where her boy was concerned. I wasn't sorry. Better she have hope, I said to myself, even though it might not last, than to have that look of dejection in those large brown eyes. With that thought I changed the subject.

"Tell me more of what the priest wrote about the Serona," I said.

I hadn't put much confidence in that manuscript. For that reason I had not pushed for information. Maybe there was still little or no reason. It was something to talk about, however—something to keep our minds off what lay ahead that night, and something to keep Janna's mind off the fate of young Christian.

"You haven't shown much interest before," she said, "but what would you like to know?"

"Does he mention why they settled in the desert?" I asked.

Of course, I understood, or thought I did, why I preferred the desert, but a whole tribe, including women and children?

"That is never mentioned," she answered, "but I imagine they chose the particular valley because of the water. Father Franciscus writes of a spring that flows from the cliff that forms the northern side of the valley. The Serona consider the water holy, magical. The gods they worship dwell in the mountain. So long as the spring flows the Serona know the gods are happy with them.

"The priest says the Serona believe that the first man and woman of the tribe were shaped and brought to life inside the mountain by the gods and sent out into the world. The valley is referred to by the Serona as Serone. Father Franciscus translates that into Spanish as meaning 'place of man.' Now I don't know that we can depend upon the manuscript. It is probably false—something Logan made up. It was a copy he brought me, written out in his own hand."

Some of the dejection shaded her voice again, and I asked, "What else did he write?"

"Had I known you had so much interest," she said, "I would have brought the manuscript along. But I was under the impression you didn't think much of it."

"Won't hurt to know what it says, just in case."

She gave me a thoughtful look.

"One of the things the manuscript says about the Serona is that when there is a marriage, the man comes to live in the house of the wife. As a result, women, and their families control the property. Descendants are kept track of through the wife's family. Wealth is passed on through her family as well."

"Sounds to me like the women have the power," I said.

"They do in such societies. In some of the eastern tribes, the women have great power. Some hold high office."

"You think that might be the case with the Serona?"

"I don't know," she answered. "Father Franciscus doesn't go into detail."

"I suppose you think young Christian stands a better chance in that case."

"That has occurred to me," she said.

"I'd like to agree, Janna. But among the Apache the women have a lot of influence, but whether they follow that custom or not, I don't know. What I do know is that Apache women can be meaner than snakes if you get them provoked. I've had some experience with them."

"I don't intend to follow up on the implications in that remark," she said, her voice tart, suggesting she was feeling better.

I felt my face warm. She had that power over me—a

look, a smile, a word from her could make me think more of myself, or less. Mostly, she had the ability to make me feel like an oversized blockhead—awkward, foolish.

As we talked, a slight breeze had sprung up. I sat there and pondered her effect on me, and felt the wind blow stronger. That is the way it is in the desert. One moment there is complete calm, and the next the wind may begin to howl. And this quickening breeze seemed insistent.

Around us was the sound of the sand as the wind picked it up and moved it along—a seething kind of sound, approximating the whir of a rattler, but more tightly wound, higher pitched. I have heard steam kettles give off something that approaches the sound, but nothing really duplicates it, nor the feeling of menace the first time you hear its steady whisper. That wind, despite the danger if it blew too strong, gave me a lift. A sensible man who keeps his wits about him can survive such a storm, and it would make our escape a whole lot easier.

I checked the heavens carefully. The sky did seem to have a high, windswept look that, strangely, brought the stars closer. A few webs of clouds gave testimony of some force up there as they scooted along, not that they promised rain. But we didn't need rain. What we needed was dust—swirling dust and sand that cuts visibility to zero.

"I'll be back in a minute," I said to Janna, my discomfiture from her remark forgotten.

I crawled over to a spot beside Levi whose eyes seemed seldom to leave Bustamente's men in the valley below. I studied them a moment myself. Bustamente had them more evenly distributed now. I counted more than five on the second front. Some were gathered about a fire. Others formed a line along the valley. I could barely make those out as the force of the wind continued to increase.

"What do you think, Levi?" I asked, sure he would know what I meant.

"I think it's going to happen, Sax," he answered.

A stronger than usual gust swept across the ridge, grabbing at my Stetson.

"I may turn into a real religious man," Levi said, and there wasn't a hint of mockery in his voice.

"Break out your rosary. It's coming," I said.

"If it does, which way'll we try to sneak out of here—to the north?"

"South," I said. "Deeper into the desert. We'll go down your side here, head east, and then cut south. I hope they think we went north. With our tracks blown away or filled with the sand, they won't be able to tell. We might give them the slip once and for all."

"By God!" Levi said, "we'll find that boy yet!"

"Bring the horses up, Levi, while I get Janna," I told him, as a shift in the wind came, causing it to strike against that side of our ridge with sufficient force to throw up a curtain of sand.

I went back for Janna, and I regretted leaving for only one reason. I still didn't know for sure who the two men were, though the size of the one strongly suggested he was Logan. The other? I hadn't a guess.

Janna came from the shadows.

"We're leaving," I said. "We'll try to slip past them down the other side of the ridge. If this keeps up, we'll stand a good chance of getting through. Are you ready to ride?"

"More than ready," she replied.

I helped her up. Later I would recall that something about her seemed a little different. But my mind was too full of the coming ride down the slope to pursue the thought then.

Standing beneath her with Levi nearby, I gave them the plan.

"You'll bring up the rear, Janna. You'll lead the pack mare. I don't need to tell you how important it is we come through with our supplies intact. Levi and I will go down first. We'll try to slip through, but if they spot us, we'll charge straight at them, kill as many as we can, and try to scatter the rest. Everybody stay close," I cautioned. "If we get scattered in this blow, we won't be able to make contact until it's over. That'll cost us a lot of valuable time."

I felt a little strange giving the strategy when Levi was in the party. He was usually the one in charge, but he didn't seem to mind. Naturally, I expected him to speak up if he disagreed.

I didn't hear the roar until I stopped talking, even then it was pitched so low and, thus, was so indistinct it hardly seemed like a sound, more like a buzzing in the back of my mind. But my scalp began to creep, and chills rippled up my spine. I had heard the sound before. Pretty soon it would grow to a ferocious howl. Overhead, the stars were already blotted out, and the moon, once bright, was now no more than a blur. The same was true of the fire below as the wind stretched it almost flat to the ground.

"Let's go," I said, and I led off.

We started slow. I wanted to save the strength of our mounts for that moment when we were spotted, if we were. Levi was to my right, spread out just enough. Glancing back, I could barely make out Janna behind, but she was there. I reached down and brought my rifle out. I saw Levi do the same.

We were halfway down, the wind grabbing at us with enough force to sweep us from the saddle in a careless moment, when two of the bandits suddenly loomed up before us. There could be only one explanation. They had decided, along with us, that the time to make a move had come. I took one out with my first shot. Levi did likewise with the other.

The two quick explosions boomed dully over the howling wind, but it was enough to converge the others on us. On the floor of the valley the fire was now no more than a faint glow, but between it and us, I saw shadows charging in our direction. I headed straight for them, hoping Levi and Janna would follow my lead.

There is no sound like the sound of a bullet as it meets head on and parts whipping sand. A shrill screech doesn't do the sound credit, and I find myself at a loss for words. But the shrill, constant scream as the rifle fire picked up mingled with the howl of the wind and the clamor and din as the wind lifted what seemed like the floor of the valley and flung it against the ridge.

We had the advantage in that charge. They were outlined, though faintly, by their fire, and we were shooting down. I saw nothing but empty saddles as the horses struggled past us. Levi emptied the last when the horse was no more than ten yards from us. At that moment I felt the moros lift up and go over the bed of coals, which still released a cascade of sparks that mingled with the whipping sand for a few feet before they were snuffed out.

The enemy seemed routed, and I pulled up. Levi came to a stop beside me. I looked for Janna.

The storm still came at us full blast. The bare skin on my face and hands felt raw from the pelting, though I hadn't been aware of it until then. Slipping my bandana up to cover my face, I peered anxiously into the swirling dust for Janna.

"What're we gonna do?" Levi shouted close in my ear.

I didn't try to answer him, but knowing he would follow, sent the moros back up the slope.

We climbed for about fifty yards in what I thought was the right direction, but there was no sign of her. In the meantime, the wind had begun to die, choking itself off as suddenly as it had begun its onslaught. I pulled the moros up, and, as visibility improved, searched frantically for movement on the slope. Not even one of the riderless horses remained, apparently already having made it over the ridge. Then the wind slowed even more, and across the valley I saw a horse. I sent the moros there in a run, Levi close behind me.

It was the pack mare, but no sign of Janna or her mount.

"They've got her," Levi said. "One of them got past us and came on her."

In his voice was a combination of anger and despair.

I was feeling the same, but I said, "Maybe not. She may have just got separated from us."

"But the pack mare is here," Levi insisted. "She would never have turned him loose. You reminded her."

"Maybe she couldn't help it," I said to him. "That's probably where she is—looking for the mare."

My first thought was to backtrack the pack mare, but within a few yards of where we found her the sign played out, covered over by the vast amount of shifting sand.

I heard a shout from the ridge then. Glancing up, I saw a line of riders perched on the edge. They had us spotted and, as I watched, they spilled over and down.

"We can't wait any longer!" Levi shouted.

He grabbed for the pack mare's rein and headed east. Reluctantly, I followed. I never left a site with heavier heart. What if she was back there on the slope buried beneath a sand dune, or lying in some hollow, hurt and in need of help? But there was nothing I could do at the moment. Bustamente's bandits were nearly on top of us.

I slowed them with a few well-placed bullets, allowing Levi, who led the pack mare, a short head start. Then I sent the moros after him.

The terrain changed as we fled, from sand dunes to granite within no time. Cliffs rose up on either side of us, split now and then by coulees and narrow canyons which at one time long ago must have been the bed of streams. Suddenly, Levi swept into one of these and pulled up.

"They won't be expecting this," he said. "They'll shoot right past us."

"I hope you're right," I told him.

"Well, if they don't, this is as good a place as any to fight it out."

"And no man I'd rather fight beside, Levi. You know that."

"Amen to that," he said.

We didn't have long to wait, and at least a dozen of them shot past the narrow mouth.

"Now, let's go back and find Janna," I said.

CHAPTER 11

THE night had now made a complete turnabout. It was hard to imagine that the serene, silent dunes about me had been, a few minutes before, a raging storm of dust and sand. The moon, now risen higher, spilled its light, by far too much light, over all—the tall cacti, with upward-pointing stovepipe limbs, a stunted Joshua tree, and the dark clumps of scattered sage. And nothing but our own movement disturbed the scene—no other sound, no other motion.

We came to the shallow valley where we had charged Bustamente's men. The place seemed undisturbed, though men had died there not an hour past. But already the wind had wiped the valley clean of that. When the sand was shifted by another storm, next month, next year, or a hundred years from now, those bodies might be uncovered again. Men would someday ride through and discover their bones and wonder about the violence that had deposited them here. I have come across such scenes in the desert myself . . . bones bleached unbelievably white, with a skull among them, the eye sockets looming startlingly black amid the white brilliance of the bones and the sand. I had stood and wondered about them.

There was no sign of Janna Dupard.

"Maybe they're holding her on the other side of the ridge," Levi said.

"Only one way to find that out," I replied, sending the moros up the slope.

The wind had swept the ridgetop free of our sign, but things were not rearranged so thoroughly as in the valley. I eased to the opposite edge and peered down. A fire burned below, and three men were gathered about it.

"The two buggers who were holding back earlier today," Levi said, "but I still can't tell if one is Logan. The third is one of Bustamente's men."

"And no sign of Janna," I said.

"You've fallen in love with the woman," Levi said, easing himself down beside me.

"Don't be foolish," I said. "The woman is our responsibility. I'm worried about her."

"Of course you are, Sax," he said. "I've noticed the way you've been mooning about, thinking of her. Don't think I haven't thought of her that way myself. 'Course, I'd never *do* anything about it. But the woman grows on you—all that money, too."

In all the years I had known him I had never heard Levi mention another woman but Amanda. I remembered the other subtle signs I had picked up on, and I recalled Amanda's concern. Something had happened to Levi in the months since I had seen him last.

He was lying alongside me now, and he let out a long sigh. "She's out there somewhere, and she's wandering about with $15,000 on her shoulder. Whoever finds her will latch onto both the money and her."

I heard the strangest quality in his voice. Turning my head, I saw the same thing reflected in his face, which I could see clearly in the moonlight. That look startled me.

"What is it, Levi?" I asked.

"All that money," he said. "I've been thinking of it a lot. I've risked my life in battles for twenty years, and I've never seen anywhere near that much. That money would mean security for me, no more worries about being shipped off to a desk in the East. I could stay here. Buy a nice ranch, stock it up, live a comfortable life."

Levi had always been a duty-first man. I had never heard him talk so. That look, and the way he sounded, made me wonder. I was thinking of that when my mind went back to the moment I had helped Janna Dupard up on her horse. The bag hadn't been on her shoulder then. That was why she had looked different to me. Then I recalled seeing her come from the shadows when I returned from speaking with Levi. She had left the bag in the shadows among the rocks.

I stood up.

"Where're you going?" Levi asked.

"Stay here. I'll be back in a minute."

I picked my way slowly along the passage that led through the boulders. In a corner in a twist of the passage, I found a pile of rocks. Kicking them aside, I discovered the bag. I picked it up and went back to where Levi waited.

"She may be wandering around out there," I said, "but she doesn't have the money. She hid it in the rocks before we rode out."

I tossed it down beside him.

He sat up quickly and took the bag. In a moment he had it open and began piling the contents to one side. He became more deliberate when he began bringing the stacks of bills out.

"You're right," he said. "She isn't wandering about with the money. We have it right here."

Levi's concern with the money bothered me, but I had known the man for years—had ridden and fought with him. You're sure you've learned all there is to know about a man after such a time. I turned my thoughts to Janna Dupard.

Had she lost sight of us in the sandstorm and got turned around—only to wander out into the desert alone? Was the explanation of her disappearance as simple as that? Or had she been picked up by Bustamente? Maybe I could find out which was true if I got close enough to the camp down there to overhear their talk. I explained what I had in mind to Levi, who offered to go with me.

"No, you stay here. If I get in trouble, come down and bail me out."

"Depend on it, Sax," he replied.

Climbing back into the saddle, I followed the ridge north a couple hundred yards. I turned west then, which took me down the slope into the center of the valley. Ahead the flames of their fire glimmered, seeming to turn the night darker. In a hollow between two dunes, I pulled the moros up and slid down. Leaving her there, I climbed the dune and stood at its crest. Between me and the fire the succession of dunes looked like waves in a sea frozen to stillness.

It was a scene that might have been taken from one of those tales of English adventurers who find themselves deep in the vast deserts of Africa, where for hundreds of miles the eye looks upon nothing but undulating lines of cresting, moonlit dunes. I had read such tales, and always their settings had seemed improbably distant—not fully credible.

Those deserts, according to the writers, bred nomads whose strength and endurance were honed by the demands of the hard existence, making them an enemy to be feared and dreaded. Would the Serona, if I ever met them, prove the same? Word had it they would.

But the three about the campfire were not Serona, though they might be as mean—meaner, if the identity of the one proved to be Logan. Being the traitor who led a woman with the wealth and power of Janna Dupard into the desert only to doublecross her would brand him as the Judas of all time. He would be hounded and hunted down in whatever country he sought refuge. He had only one choice: make sure none of us ever got back to name him.

The adage that haste makes waste was never more true than in the desert. Many men have not survived to learn that. I had. I observed it now, though I expected that at any moment the three about the fire might be joined by the dozen bandits who were out chasing Levi and me. Despite that thought, I worked my way slowly from dune to dune, using the back side to make up for the cautious descent of the side facing the fire. Finally, I found myself peering over the crest of the last dune that separated me from their camp.

I thought I was prepared for the man to turn out to be Logan. Maybe I was. Maybe it was the identity of the other that left me in a state of shock, for beside Baxter Logan sat none other than Richard Farley!

Richard Farley who professed to love Janna Dupard, who had convinced me of his love. The same man who had argued so forcefully that the venture should never be attempted.

Actually, the first thing that popped into my mind was that Logan had managed to take Farley prisoner and had forced him along, but he sat there as free as a bird, and from the holster worn outside that stylish outfit the butt of a six-gun protruded. Farley was in this business up to his teeth. There was no other explanation.

There is no man I despise more than one who brings about the downfall of a friend. Such a man takes advantage of trust and affection, using those fine attributes as a shield from behind which he schemes and plots, but to use love for a fine woman as a shield was even more contemptible. There sat Farley, the best friend of a dead man, taking a hand in the betrayal of the dead man's wife, and God only knew what else they had in mind. I can't describe the anger and disgust that stirred me.

The icing on the cake for the double cross, so to speak, were the times Farley had argued so forcefully of the dangers of such a trip. Those arguments, I believe, were what finally convinced me of his sincerity. But it had all been a game of charades. I recalled that Logan had always got in the last shot, with Farley quietly acquiescing. I vowed on the spot to do everything in my power to see that they paid dearly for the scheme.

I was still too far from the camp to overhear their talk, and there was no way I could get closer from that side without being discovered. To get closer I would have to circle to the south and come up on the camp again. That would take time, and I had the feeling time was running out on me. Bustamente had to have given up the chase by now—had to be on his way back in. Still, I didn't see that I had much choice. I slid back down to the bottom of the dune and cut to the west.

I could hear their voices beyond as I eased up the final pile of sand. I guess I got overanxious and forgot that first law of the desert: when there is a choice, always go slow. Maybe I didn't see the rattler because his color turned him into what appeared to be no more than a ripple in the sand—until I heard the dry whir of his rattles. He was within three feet of my face, and I watched as he drew himself into a coil to strike.

I know about the poor eyesight all snakes are supposed to possess—that they locate the victim by testing the air with their tongues, but the moonlight caught his dull gaze, and I would swear he looked straight into my eyes. From that distance, who knows?

He was near enough for me to catch his odor—a dusty, dry smell which, in my imagination, seemed to represent all the dangers of the desert. On the other hand, I might have been catching a whiff of my own fear.

We faced a ticking stalemate—me and the snake, with every passing tick reminding me that my time was running out on two fronts. If I continued to lie there, the bandits would certainly return, but that might not be of any consequence to me if the snake decided to make a leaping strike.

I had to move, but I had to do it without alarming the snake, and just beyond the sand dune were Logan and Farley, so near I could hear the drone of their voices. A crunch of the sand might bring them down on me.

Ever so carefully and slowly, I began to inch my way back, pressing my forearms softly against the sand to gain leverage, and pulling with my toes, willing myself back, but all the while keeping my eyes on the snake for the first indication he was ready to launch himself.

I had gained maybe six inches when that deadly whir ceased, and I sensed he was gathering for the leap. I didn't continue to push backward then. Instead, I rolled. The snake came down just short of where my face had been.

I don't recall making a sound, but I must have grunted or yelled something, however.

"What was that?" I heard Logan ask. Then in Spanish he ordered the Mexican up the dune to find out.

By then the snake was wriggling away in the darkness.

But there was no time for me to retreat. Beyond the crest of sand, I heard the Mexican as he climbed. I moved quickly up and waited, my knife in my hand. When his head appeared, I grabbed him.

I brought him down on top of me, one hand over his mouth as I slipped my knife neatly between his ribs. His only sound was a terrified grunt, which was muffled by my hand. He kicked a couple of times as I cleaned my knife on his shirt.

Whether Logan and Farley heard that grunt, I don't know. Maybe they did, or maybe they only sensed that something was wrong.

"Garcia!" Logan called, "you find anything?"

The silence that followed seemed to fill with their growing apprehension.

"Where the hell are you, Garcia?" Logan called again.

Another silence followed, shorter this time, and definitely reflecting the growing fear of the two.

"Get up there, Farley, and see what happened to him!" Logan ordered.

That surprised me almost as much as seeing Farley earlier—Logan giving the orders. I suppose I had expected that the scheme would have been hatched in the mind of Farley—that he would have been in charge. Somehow the fact that he wasn't disappointed me. That may sound strange, but the thought came from my feeling that there was even more to despise in a man who had turned traitor to a friend to serve a scoundrel like Logan. From where I lay beside the dead Mexican, I heard Farley begin his climb up.

Well, it had worked once, why not try again, I asked myself, and I eased into position.

Farley came more cautiously than the Mexican, however. An eternity seemed to pass before I caught a whiff of that well-barbered scent and saw his head, every hair still in place, rise above the crest of the dune.

I reached for him, but I didn't bring him down as easily as I had the Mexican. In the first place, he was a lot heavier. Secondly, he was on his guard, and he grabbed for me at about the same time. We rose up atop the dune as we struggled.

I managed to knock his feet from beneath him and sent him face down into the sand, and I slammed his head deeper with a foot to his neck. But I had forgotten about Logan. I heard his gun explode and felt the bullet fan the air near my face. I forgot about Farley then and grabbed for my own gun as Logan got another shot off, the bullet stinging my side as it nipped me.

Logan was clearly outlined by the fire, and I tried not to hurry my shot. I squeezed the trigger and watched him jarred backward straight into the fire. When he came down, he lay across the edge of the flame. He was dazed, I suppose, for he lay there a moment as the fire caught his clothes. Then his scream split the desert night. He rolled from the fire, a move he should have continued, but he didn't. Instead, he came to his feet and began to run.

I didn't get to follow that drama, however. I had to return to Farley. I had caught a single glimpse of him during the exchange of shots with Logan. He had brought his head from the sand; but his eyes, nose, and mouth had been clogged. Gagging, spitting, scratching, he had been struggling to get his breath and his vision. I guess he managed, because, as I turned from my last glimpse of the fleeing Logan, Farley rammed into me head-on and from above me on the dune. I locked onto him with my arms, and together we tumbled down the dune, each of us working to gain advantage over the other.

He landed on top.

I have told of what a physical specimen Farley was. I

found out now that someone, during that pampered life, had taught him how to fight. Maybe he picked it up at Harvard or Princeton College. I had read that those were the schools rich boys preferred—that they went in for boxing and wrestling there. If that's where Farley picked it up, they taught him to fight for keeps.

He rammed a knee into my crotch first off. The next moment his fingers locked together to form a double fist which he smashed into my face. Fireworks exploded in my head, and the showering display seemed to join up with the torture from my groin in a celebration of pain.

For what seemed like a long time, but which, in reality, could have been only seconds, the celebration continued. Then I began to fight back the fog. Even in the midst of the pain I had continued to fight—kicking, scratching, clawing—anything to keep Farley from finishing me off, reflexive actions from one who had fought all his life, I suppose. But Farley still held me down.

His face was just above me, lit by the fire. I saw a mixture of hate and fear in his eyes. His face reflected the same emotions, and from his mouth came some of the vilest language I have ever heard.

I swung a blow to the side of his head, striking the soft part of the temple. I saw the effects of it in his eyes, but the result was to stir him to greater effort. He brought the double fist down into my face again, seeming to crush my nose. I struck at his temple again, and the blow seemed to make him wild. His hands came apart and circled my throat.

I tried to twist and roll from beneath him, but his legs were locked onto me, squeezing me like a cowboy astride a bronc.

In a last desperate attempt to get free, I swung my legs

up, wrapped them about his face, and locked my ankles. Giving it all my strength, I brought my legs down. He didn't let go at once, and it became a test of strength, his hands about my throat, my legs locked onto his face. Then I felt his hands give, and with a final effort I flipped him backward.

The air I sucked in seemed to scorch my throat, and I lay there for a brief second, trying not to die and gradually filling the black void which had been forming somewhere in the back of my head.

We came up at about the same time. Farley, instead of coming toward me, was backing away, his hand searching for the six-gun in what was now an empty holster. All of a sudden he seemed to understand that he had lost the gun in the struggle. A desperate look flashed into his face, then something else, and I saw his hand streak for one of those big pockets. It came out holding an ugly little snub-nosed derringer—a two-shot gun, unless I was seeing double as I stared into the pea-sized bore.

I knew my own holster was empty from the feel of it on my hip, and I never carried a backup gun. I thought of my knife, but I couldn't recall having it since Farley and I had hurtled down the sand dune. Then I caught the gleam of its blade in the sand between me and the fire. But there was no chance I could get to it before Farley pulled the trigger of the derringer.

A lot of men carry those little backup weapons. Gamblers sometime carry nothing else because they are easily hidden. Except at close range, they aren't very accurate. But I was quite close, and Farley's bullet struck my shoulder with a jolt. I didn't wait. I made a desperate dive into the sand for my knife. I came up with it, and Farley, waiting for a second shot, and trying to make it a good one, took too long. I threw the knife at his chest. He squeezed the shot off as a reaction to the feel of the blade going in.

He dropped the gun, and his hands went to his chest, as though he thought to pull the blade out. But he changed his mind, fingering the handle almost fondly. Then, his hands still on the handle, he sank to the sand and lay down.

I crawled over to where he lay, hoping there was still time for me to get some information out of him.

"You haven't much time, Farley. Tell me one thing. Do you have any idea where Janna is?"

He was dying, but that got his attention. He twisted his head so he could look at me. The fire cast its light into his face. I saw in his eyes the most desperate fear of all—the fear of a man who knows he is dying and who knows he faces certain perdition, if there is any god at all.

"You . . . you don't know where she is?" he asked.

"We got separated in the storm," I said. "I thought maybe Bustamente's men might have found her."

"No," he said, already getting weaker.

"Why, Farley?" I asked. "Why did you doublecross her?"

"The money . . ." he whispered. "I had a bad run—gambling, some ventures gone bad. I needed it to keep my head above the water."

"My God, man! Why didn't you just ask for it! She was a friend. She would have given it to you."

"No," he whispered, "Old Campost controls all the money. Since Yancey's death he's been afraid I might get my hands on some of it. He locked it all up in a trust for the boy. Janna can't touch it."

"The boy? Is there anything to that story?"

"Yes."

"You mean he's alive? That he actually is a captive of the Serona?"

"Yes. Logan's visit was legitimate—to bring news of the boy. I think he had this plan in his mind all along, though. He needed my help, and I saw a chance to recoup some of my losses."

I felt sick to my stomach. I wanted to take the knife and puncture him again. I was saved the trouble. He died.

I sat there in the sand beside my second corpse of the night. My shoulder throbbed like hell, and I wondered where Levi was. Surely he had seen from the ridge what was taking place in the camp.

But I couldn't sit there and figure out why he hadn't come down to help. Bustamente and his men were already long overdue. I did take time for a glance at my shoulder. Pulling my shirt back, I saw the crease Farley's bullet had plowed across the skin. It was still bleeding, but it wasn't a serious wound.

Three oversized canteens lay about the fire. I took those. There was plenty of food as well, and I would have taken some of that had I known what was ahead. But I didn't know. I pulled my knife from Farley's chest, cleaned it, and looked around for my Colt. I found it halfway down the sand dune. I wiped it free of sand, stuck it in its holster, and headed for the hollow where I had left the mare.

I kept a lookout for Logan, because he had run in that direction, and I thought I might have the pleasure of coming across his charred remains. I didn't find him, however.

I gave the mare a shot of the water, holding a canteen above her upturned head and pouring the water down her throat. She had taken water from a canteen before and knew how to do it. I took a shot of the water, too.

I sent the moros up the slope, and we were working our way along the ridge to where I had left Levi, when Bustamente and his men rode into the camp below. They buzzed around down there like hornets around their nest after it's been disturbed. I didn't pay them too much attention. Mostly I was wondering where the hell Levi was.

I pulled up at the spot which I was getting to know pretty well by then and looked around for Levi. Unless he was hiding in the rocks, he was gone.

I called for him softly several times, even searching along the passage where I had found the money. Then I checked the slope away from the fire below, the one Levi and I had climbed together a short time back. I found our sign, and I found some more as well—two horses going down. Levi's geld and the pack mare? I couldn't be sure, because the tracks had filled with sand. But I backtracked them to the ridge and found prints in more solid ground. They were prints I knew almost as well as I did the prints of my mare. They led down the slope and across the dunes. Levi had taken the money and the pack mare and rode off and left me.

That left me with a decision to make—ride after Levi, talk some sense into him, and bring him back, or try to find Janna Dupard. There was no contest. Whatever had possessed Levi he would have to deal with himself—and suffer the consequences. I intended to find Janna and give her the word about her boy.

CHAPTER 12

I SPENT the rest of that night hidden in a twisting passage of lava bed, whose floor was softened a bit by the sand which had blown in. I didn't sleep much. My mind was too full of the things I had just found out.

Logan's treachery didn't come as much of a surprise, but Farley's hand in the scheme left me baffled. I doubt that I'll ever understand it. I suppose greed may have cast its evil spell upon him. If that is the explanation, it dealt swiftly with a hollow heart, and turned Farley into a pariah. He was dead now, hollow heart and all, and the desert had claimed another trophy.

And there was Levi.

Of all the men I have known, I would have said Levi would be the last to be lured from his duty by the greed for money. As I lay there and looked back over the years I had known him, I toyed with the idea there had to be some other explanation—that one of Bustamente's men might have captured him. Or that, thinking me dead, he had fled in order to search for Janna. I couldn't escape the truth, however, when I recalled the sound in his voice, not to mention the look on his face, when he was fondling the money. There was only one conclusion. Levi had taken the money and deserted me.

I thought of Amanda and felt sick. How could I tell her that Levi had turned into a thief? She had been so troubled over the trip—her concern, I had thought, having to do with some sort of fascination Levi had for Janna. Now I wondered if that had been it at all. Maybe she knew of the money somehow. Maybe Levi had known, and all along the temptation of it was the source of her worry.

That it all had something to do with Levi's being shipped off back East to what amounted to retirement was certain. The prospects had unraveled Levi. It is hard for old warriors to lay down their weapons. Harder still, I should think, when they have commanded the fighting.

When I woke, the sun was in my face, and the nose of the moros was nuzzling my chest. She was telling me the time had come for us to travel. The first thing I did was give her a handful of the grain and a half-canteen of the scarce water. I could hardly miss the gauntness in her sides. She needed a good graze, and more water than I could give her if I poured every drop in the canteens down her throat.

But I couldn't delay my search for Janna longer to search for grass and water. Searching for water in the desert is a chancy thing at best. It isn't something you set out on a straight line for. Luck is everything, and unintentional wandering is as good as setting a course. I would pray for luck and search for Janna and water at the same time, depending much on the keen nose of the moros.

The first step of my search for Janna had to be to try and locate her trail. The surest way to do that, I decided, was to make a circle of the valley in which she had become separated from us, since I could hardly just ride back and pick up her trail, with Bustamente and his men still hanging about. If I didn't find her sign somewhere along the circle, I would know she was still in or very near the valley. Of course, evading the bandits might prove as difficult as finding Janna's trail.

I had to contend with the heat as well. Ordinarily, I

don't mind desert heat. The dry air makes it tolerable to me, and I'm used to it. But somehow it strikes at you differently when you are being pushed, or it seems different. Lazing along you're hardly aware of it, but once set upon a purpose with a time limit, it becomes a hindrance— especially when you're aboard a mount in need of water and feed.

It was a blazing heat, the sun overhead glaring and dazzling. And it launched an attack even upon the air, turning the horizons into twisting, taunting devil dancers, and the sand into a sizzling, white grill. And all the while the precious liquids remaining in the moros were being squeezed from her by an effort I had no choice but to command—squeezed out and snatched up quickly by the voracious thirst of the desert air and heat.

We rode for some time before I saw the mare's ear switch forward into an alert. I checked the horizon for signs of movement and dust. Nothing there but the dancers. Then she veered to the left, tightening the circle we were making. I let her go. That nose had saved us both a few times before. I was hoping for just one more time.

Even when you are lucky enough to stumble upon it, desert water can be a deadly drink. There is arsenic in the desert, more than you might think, and water oozing through sand and rock can become laced with the poison. The result is a killing brew, and even the air above the spring can be turned into a gaseous executioner. I have seen birds flying over such springs drop dead in flight. Sometimes the water, a nasty color, reflects its deadliness. The sand and rocks it touches become coated with the slime. But often the water has the look of purity and only to the taste may seem slightly wrong. That water is the most dangerous to stumble upon when a man, or an animal, is dying of thirst.

The mare came to a stop, appearing uncertain for a moment about the direction of the drifting scent. Then she turned down a slight slope into a depression whose floor was studded with boulders and protruding slabs of dark granite. She found the water in the middle of these, a seepage which spread a circle of dampness for several yards among the granite and the boulders. Among the passages separating these, the sand supported some thin-bladed grass—not much, but enough for the mare to fill out her sides some. The water itself covered a space a little larger than a tub.

The moros sniffed it tentatively. Next she lowered her lips into it a little and took a sip or two. She seemed satisfied the water was fit to drink, but I slid from the saddle and kept her from drinking more until I tested it myself.

The sulphur smell wasn't unusual for the desert and didn't bother me. Better still, there were no remains of small animals about. I knelt, dipped a finger in, and stuck it in my mouth. The sulphur was strong, which could mask something else, but I didn't think so. The moros agreed. She wanted more.

"All right, if that's your judgment," I said.

I gave her a loose rein. She drank moderately. Turning from the water, she began to clip the grass, her judgment rendered. I combined the water I had left into one canteen and filled the rest. Then I stretched out on the damp sand and drank myself.

Meanwhile, the mare clipped the grass. I let her harvest what there was, and brought her back for another drink. She took more this time before she went back to nibble at what remained of the grass stems.

I wet my bandana and swabbed the dust from my face

and neck. Any other time I might have stayed long enough for a bath and shave, but Janna Dupard was still out there somewhere alone. So were the bandits out there, and they could cover a lot more ground than I could if they decided to split up.

The moros took a final drink, and I climbed up. I put her back on the circle we were executing before she caught scent of the water. A mile or so away from the depression I stopped to note landmarks in case I needed to return.

A short time later I crossed the tracks of two horses heading south. It is difficult to read the age of dry, sandy prints. They are always indistinct, but I felt sure I was looking at tracks laid down the night before—about the time Levi would have ridden through. In that southward direction lay Mexico City. Was that his destination? Fifteen thousand dollars would last a while down there.

Would he ever contact Amanda? If he did, what would he say to her? Would she consent to join him? Such questions were imponderables for which I had no answers.

I pushed on, fighting the heat, and keeping an eye out for Bustamente's men. I remember giving a thought or two to Logan, wondering if he had died, either from my bullet or the burns he had picked up from the flames. My judgment was that the shot would prove fatal, if not the burns, but he had skipped across the sand dunes in a lively fashion. Maybe he had survived. But I wished him dead, writhing in lonely pain in the middle of the desert night. He deserved that and more.

I had executed most of the circle when I came on the second set of tracks—tracks put down by one horse, traveling south as well, but not in the direction of Mexico City. More to the southeast—in fact, deeper into that empty space on Levi's map, into the heart of the area where we had hoped to make contact with the Serona.

It had to be Janna. She had sat and studied that map with me. She had noted time after time that southeasterly direction. Finding herself separated from us, she had struck out in that direction on her own.

Again the age of the sign was hard to read. There had been little if any wind, yet the sides of the prints had caved in, filling the punched-out impressions with dribbled-in sand. I guessed again that the prints had been left the night before, which meant, if that was correct, she was several hours ahead of me. Glancing about for telltale signs of trailing dust from the bandits, and seeing none, I set out on what I was convinced was Janna's trail.

A slight wind soon sprang up—not enough to cover the tracks, but enough to send the sand swirling in spurts from time to time a few inches from the ground. Here and there were stunted Joshua palm and greasewood, and always the sand, the rocks, and the sage. At times the wind brushed these, producing those soft and seductive sounds heard only in deserts—enchanting lullabies of death if the listener lowers his guard.

Gradually, the terrain underwent a change. The sand was left behind and the passage grew more rugged. I passed from dunes to a land of cliffs and flat-topped mesas, from those to a land of rugged canyons and tall, stark peaks. Molten lava filled the passes, making tracking more difficult.

I kept on, finding an overturned stone here and a chalky break there, even a print from time to time in some slight hollow which had become filled with sand. Not much of a trail, but there to be followed if the eyes were sharp. But the tracking was slow. I had the feeling I was being left further and further behind, and my concern grew.

Naturally, I feared she would be found first by the

bandits, even by the Serona—but I feared for more as well. I recalled the half-empty canteen she had carried, and her only food had been the small wrap of jerky I had placed in each rider's saddlebags. The jerky would last a day or two, but the water was a different matter. There was not enough to keep Janna alive, and her mare would be suffering thirst as well.

I remembered explaining to her that the advantage of riding a mustang into the desert was the animal's ability to locate water. Maybe she would remember that and give the mare her head—let the horse save her, as the moros had me more than a few times. If she didn't trust the horse, I would find both rider and mount dying of thirst along one of the rocky passes. Still, worry though I might, all I could do was push on.

Night came, and I had no choice but to stop.

Feeding into the broader canyon I was following were smaller, narrower passes. I turned the moros into one of these, looking for a spot that offered more protection than the open spaces of the canyon.

I was barely into the narrow coulee when the mare stopped suddenly with a snort. She danced a bit and took a step or two backward. Directly before her I saw the cause for her alarm—a rattler the size of my arm. He was coiled defiantly, rattles whirring.

I slid from the saddle and picked up a rock. Speaking reassuringly to the moros, I stepped toward the snake. The rock was heavy enough to crush his head if I hit him right.

He must have caught my scent or movement, because he switched the point of his head in my direction. I slammed the rock down on him, pinning the head. He writhingly uncoiled, flipped about for a time, and died.

The mare didn't take well to my climbing back into the saddle with the snake in my hand. Only seldom did our judgments clash, and I had to speak soothingly to her several times. Finally, she relented.

A hundred yards further into the narrowing crack, I found a cave. Before its entrance grew some stunted mesquite. About the ground were scattered a few dead limbs, more than enough for my fire. I pulled the mare up and stepped down.

Darkness was upon me, so I gathered the limbs quickly. But before I laid the fire I saw to the moros. I stripped her of gear first. Then I tore off the corner of my blanket, wet it with a dribble of the milky water, and swabbed her down, cleaning her coat of dust and salty sweat. After a handful of grain and a half-canteen of water, I staked her near the entrance of the cave. She knelt down and took a wallow despite the rubdown I had given her.

I built my fire deep enough into the cave to keep it from being seen. The aroma of burning mesquite was strong. That concerned me, but I wanted to roast the snake meat.

I stripped the skin away quickly and peeled the white flesh from the long stretch of backbone and needle-like ribs. Roasted over the mesquite, its taste was sweet and delicious, a marvelous treat for a growling appetite, and a present from the desert.

I wasn't the first to visit that cave. Charcoal from a very old fire littered the floor. The ceiling had a few dark smudges from smoke. I studied these signs, and then something prompted a cautious glance into the darkness at the back of the hollow. Not much light penetrated that darkness, but I thought I caught a reflection. My edginess turned up a notch, and I dropped my hand to my Colt.

The silence in the dimly lit cave was broken only by an

occasional sizzle from the burning mesquite, and despite the aroma of the burning wood, I picked up a musty smell, the smell of undisturbed ages that beckoned me toward the back of the cave.

I stuck a fresh limb into the fire and got it burning. With this as a torch, I moved cautiously into the cave. Something from the back caught the light of the torch and cast dull, winking gleams back at me—something that leaned against the rocky wall. My scalp seemed to crawl a little, and my spine shivered. I slipped the Colt from its holster.

I thought bear, then puma, imagining their eyes sizing me up from the darkness as an explanation of the reflection I had seen. Then I remembered that neither of those animals was to be found in desert country such as this, and the glow had not come from eyes—much too dull. Then what? There was only one way to find out, and, step after cautious step, I went nearer.

I stopped a few feet short and stared down at what seemed a hooded figure who sat with his back to the wall. I almost spoke, but the round, pointed shape of that head fell into place for me. I was staring at a Spanish helmet that rested atop a suit of armor.

I let loose a slightly nervous chuckle and reholstered the old Colt. Kneeling before the thing, I lowered my torch for a look into the face within the helmet. A skull grinned back at me, the dark sockets forming terrible eyes. I had to hold myself there. Then a small lizard eased from one of the sockets as I watched. He saw the light and flipped back into the skull. I retreated.

I had intended to sleep in the cave, but I changed my mind. I bedded down outside within a few steps of the mare, grateful for her company.

I tried not to think of my grisly discovery, but that proved impossible, of course. What were the circumstances which had led him to this cave to die alone? The Spanish who wore such armor would have preceded Father Franciscus by a hundred or so years. Had he been wounded in a fight with the Serona? Fleeing, had he found the cave and crawled in to die?

Or had he been brought down by disease and left there by comrades? Many Spanish had died of diseases caught from the Indians. The opposite had been the case as well. The first scourges of cholera and plague on the new continent had been brought over on Spanish ships.

More imponderables. At first light of dawn, I was up and on the trail, anxious to be free of that unhappy gorge.

Now the sign was even more scarce—an infrequent scrape here, a mark there. Then it played out completely. I wasn't too concerned, knowing that the broad canyon offered Janna the only real choice. She would know that the shootoffs led nowhere but to dead ends.

The country grew more rugged still, and it was still desert, mountain desert—naked, towering peaks of various hues of brown. Now there was nothing that resembled a tree, no chink or crack in the rock in which enough silt might gather to support even a blade or two of grass—just desolate, dark rock that rang as the iron shoes of the moros struck it, and overhead the jagged crags, and to each side the cliffs and, now and then, a narrow, twisting canyon.

And it was hot, relentlessly hot, hotter than on the sand dunes, and not a breath of wind stirred. The poet Milton, blind, composing his epic poem *Paradise Lost,* must have had such a place in mind as the battlefield where Satan made his stand against God.

Silence is the companion of the desert, and I like nothing better. But this was different—a silence that was more than silence; something ominous, menacing.

I rode on.

Then I was served up a predicament. The canyon split about the base of a towering peak. Two canyons led on, and I had to decide which to take. I searched from side to side across the mouth of both, but there was no indication that a horse had entered either.

Maybe I had outguessed myself when I had first lost the trail. Maybe Janna had ridden into one of the offshoots—like the Spaniard, looking for a place to die. The thought filled me with a sense of loss.

Until that moment I don't think I had allowed myself to consider what Janna Dupard had come to mean to me. I had known many women but had never grown to love one, and this sudden revelation filled me with awe, and a great longing to see her alive—once more, at least.

I considered retracing the canyon, searching the mouth of each offshoot pass, until I rediscovered her trail, but something in me argued against it. Surely, if she had any strength left, she would have continued on, and I recalled the last time we had spoken of young Christian, expressing renewed hope about his being alive. No, she had gone on and had entered one of these two canyons.

Sighting by the sun, I chose the canyon that most nearly kept to the direction we had followed since entering Mexico. My choice made, I pushed on.

Eventually, the canyon narrowed. As the walls gradually closed in on me, I began to think I had chosen a dead end. On the one hand, I didn't find that completely bad. If Janna had followed the same canyon, and I felt strongly that she had, I would find her up there.

I asked the moros for a little more speed. She had some left.

What appeared to be a dead end turned out to be no more than a sharp, twisting turn. I stopped in the elbow and stared ahead at more of the same: a rocky split in the earth, a hundred yards or so wide in places, in others only half as much. And as far as I could see, nothing moved.

I believe I might even have welcomed the canyon dead-ending there—if I had found Janna. I had been riding between those walls of stone for several days, though I seemed to have lost count of how many. The monotony of the landscape—the uninterrupted silence, the almost total absence of life—had a tendency to merge one day and night into another. I was rationing my food and water as well, saving most of the water for the moros, and I was beginning to feel some of the effects—chiefly, a little lightheadedness from time to time.

Then, miracle of miracles, there was a change! The ring of the mare's shoes on the stone floor became duller. Glancing down, I discovered the rocky floor was now covered with a thin layer of black soil. Next, I saw a few sprigs of yellow grass, and a hundred yards further on a stunted tree—a very small, runty one, but a tree nonetheless.

I pulled up at once. I could now search the canyon floor for some sign that Janna had preceded me.

I turned for the wall to my right first, checking every inch for a mark or scrape in the strange looking black dirt. There had been no wind to wipe out a trail that I could remember. If she had been along there, I would find her sign.

The only sign I found, however, was the twisting path of a rattler who had pulled himself along through the black sand—nothing else between me and the cliff wall. I turned around and headed for the other side to search.

I found the tracks a few feet out from the opposite cliff, as though she had chosen to ride there to stay in the shade of the cliff. There could be no mistake. I stared down at a print that was familiar to me. I had seen that print many times over the last few weeks. The mustang I had selected for Janna had put down the trail.

But I couldn't tell much about how old the trail was. As with prints left in desert sand, there was no moisture to dry out. The prints might have been made an hour ago, yesterday, or the day before, but one thing was encouraging: Very little dust had drifted into them, which might mean they were fresh. That was a fragile hope, for there had been no wind, as I have mentioned.

Finding that trail picked my spirits up. I now knew that Janna wasn't dead—that she was somewhere up ahead of me. But immediately after that encouraging thought I had another that sent me worrying again as the sprigs of yellow grass increased and the runty trees grew more numerous. Was I seeing the first signs of an inhabited land? Had I entered the land of the Serona? And Janna was somewhere up ahead of me, of course.

And the heat had not abated—far from it. In fact, the black soil seemed to catch the heat and hold on to it even more than desert sand, turning the temperature higher. There might be a few scraggly trees and some stretches of grass, but I still rode through an inferno, an inferno with mountains that grimaced at me from the distance, sometimes appearing to writhe and wriggle all over the horizon.

But I soon noticed a difference. Not so much in the heat, but in the way I was sweating. My sweat formed into drops, and it remained longer before the dry air sucked it up, some even collecting to run down my face. A few spirals of steam drifted up from the wet neck of the mare as well.

The humidity was increasing!

I pulled the mare up and studied the canyon. I had been too busy concentrating on the trail before to notice it, but the floor of the canyon was descending, almost imperceptably. I turned and peered back the way I had come. There was some rise. I had been descending for some time.

Then in the distance I spotted trees! Tall trees, a dozen or more, and beneath them grass—dark, deep green in color!

Trees! Here in this place. A small grove of them! And enough grass for a whole herd of horses!

I repeated those words to myself over and over—maybe whispered them aloud, so filled was I with wonder from the sight. Then the thought that I might be seeing a mirage hit me. Most of my desert mirages have space between them and the ground. I searched for that line of space, but I didn't find it. Then I closed my eyes and shook my head a couple of times. When I looked again, the trees were still unmistakably there. The moros gave a couple of impatient stamps to indicate she had had enough lallygagging—that the time had come to move on. I gave her the signal.

The steps of Janna's mare lengthened after that. The thought occurred to me that Janna had spotted the trees at about the same point I had. Of course, her mare might have caught the scent of water, as the moros was giving some signs of doing. Janna's mount had been a long time without water. That could explain the longer stride. Janna could be clinging to the saddle, barely alive. Without food or water for so long, it seemed a good bet.

The thought struck me then that if there was water among the trees, Janna would have chosen to spend some time there—to rest up, and let her horse get some rest as well. Still, and despite that thought, I approached with some caution.

The silence, as I moved up, was still pervasive, but I did catch sight of something I had not seen for days. A cluster of vultures circled high overhead, drifting lightly on currents of some wind. Vultures stick close to living things, I thought to myself—living things that die, furnishing them with food. I didn't take the thought any further. Maybe the same wind the vultures were riding dipped down to stir the trees, as I then caught the sound and heard the snap of wind-whipped cottonwood leaves.

The tracks of Janna's mare led beneath the cottonwood. I followed, taking my time, ears and eyes open. I was watching the moros as well. She would give some sign when she caught the scent of the mustang.

Before me in a spot clear of trees, I came upon a pile of the black dirt, as though someone had dug there. I eased the moros close enough to see that such was indeed the case.

Then it struck me. Not finding surface water, Janna had begun to dig to find the water underneath—the water that fed the cottonwoods. I was impressed. Any westerner knows that where you find cottonwood you find water, though there is never any guarantee how close to the surface it will be. But Janna had known that somewhere down there was water, and she had begun to dig for it.

But what had happened to interrupt the digging?

I slid from the saddle and stepped closer. I saw more prints then, bare footprints. They came from behind a large boulder at the foot of the cliff to the hole. Just beyond the hole there had been a struggle. Janna had, apparently, climbed from the hole to meet them. Then the struggle. . . .

There was a scrambled mess of prints that led away from the hole, as though Janna was still fighting. I followed along, leading the moros.

Further along, maybe forty yards or so, I found the hat Janna had worn. It was ground into the sand as though someone had stepped on it and then given a twist of their foot. I picked the hat up and pushed the crown straight. Soon I came to the spot where horses had been tethered. I counted at least seven. These, with the prints of Janna's mustang among them, led south.

Janna had made contact, finally, with the Serona. Or they with her. No doubt about it. I hoped she had been able to overcome the suspicions they would surely have, and that she had got through to them. Otherwise, I might never find her alive.

Satisfied I couldn't be too far from water now, I gave the moros a healthy swig from my last canteen. When she had drunk, I took a sip or two myself.

But I didn't kill any time. Glancing at the sun, I figured I had at most two hours until dark. I wanted to get close in to the Serona village before darkness fell.

CHAPTER 13

I WAS following at least seven horses. The ground was all churned up, making the job easy. The prints of Janna's mare were easy to distinguish, since the others were un-shod. That told me a little about those who had taken her captive—that they were probably Indians and not Busta-mente's men. Those bare footprints suggested more. Were the Serona so primitive they went about in rattler-infested country with no protection for their legs and feet?

I figured to know the answer to that question soon enough, because in the middle of it I caught the smell of woodsmoke.

The walls of the canyon had begun to flatten out by then. What had been sheer cliffs were turning into tree-lined slopes. I saw pine, some hardwood, and, lower down, some cottonwood and willow. Animal life picked up as well. There were rabbits and grouse on the ground and plenty of birds in the trees. Hard to believe I had been riding through a land empty of most life a few hours earlier.

What made the difference?

The only explanation I came up with was that the altitude had lowered considerably. Maybe in eons past something deep inside the earth had exploded, throwing up a vast belt of mountainous lava around the valley. Heat from a blazing sun, a rocky floor on which the wind had allowed no silt to collect, and the resulting quick runoff of any rain had turned the surrounding country into desert.

This sunken valley, which had benefited from that drainage, no doubt, was probably low enough to tap into some underground moisture as well, and I recalled what the priest had written about the flow of sacred water from a northern cliff.

At the smell of smoke, caution became even more my watchword. I kept to the best cover, which proved to be a line of trees along the northeast side of the valley, causing me to have to desert the tracks I had been following until then. I was picking my way as quietly as I could through the thickest of the trees when, suddenly, I heard a dog bark. That was followed by the squeals of what sounded like playing children.

I pulled up.

The barks continued, as did the sound of the children, and through the treetops I saw smoke curling up. I was within two hundred yards of the village, I estimated, but I still hadn't caught sight of a house.

I decided the solution was to work my way to higher ground. The dog helped me to make that decision. Most Indians keep dogs about their villages. Before they got horses from the Spanish, they used dogs as transport. They also ate them, which many still do. In the beginning, they kept the sturdiest out of their pots, because they could haul more. Since the advent of horses, the dogs that escaped the pots most frequently were those who were the best watchdogs, and that made getting in close to a village without alarming the dogs a thing that was almost impossible to do. Higher up, I wouldn't run the risk of having the dogs pick up my scent, and I would be able to see the layout of the village, possibly spotting where Janna was kept, or so I hoped.

I sent the moros up the slope.

The cover remained good, and the climb was not difficult. The most trouble came from the covering of dead
leaves. They can be slick, doubly so when climbing. The
noise as the mare's hoofs scattered them was a little loud
as well.

I topped out on a shoulder several yards wide and about
halfway up the slope. There was less cover, but the thick
carpet of grass muffled any sound. The grass got the
attention of the moros, since she hadn't fed well of late. I
was tempted to pull up and let her feed awhile, but I
noticed the thickest, greenest grass grew nearest the base
of the slope. That meant seepage. If I was lucky, I might
find water to go with the grass further on.

I did. Within fifty yards, a small gurgle that formed a
pool no bigger than a frypan. I pulled up and slid from
the saddle. I gave myself a good stretch as the horse drank.
Then she took to the grass without asking any permission
from me, clipping at it hungrily. She would need several
bellyfuls, however, before she regained the weight the
desert had melted from her.

I stretched out, belly down, and drank myself. The
water was sweet and pure. When I was finished, I refilled
the canteens, taking time to rinse them free of the taste of
the milky water from the desert spring. Then, leaving the
mare on the grass, I made my way to the edge of the
shoulder.

I had a surprisingly good view of the village. Stretched
beneath the low branches of an oak, only the sharp eye of
someone purposefully studying the top would see me. I
relaxed and began a careful survey of the village and its
layout.

The houses were primitive. They appeared no more
than square huts constructed of rough limbs, their roofs

thatched with grass. I was reminded of the huts of the temporary villages of renegade Apaches who had fled from their reservations across the Rio Grande—temporary abodes, thrown together from whatever was at hand, mostly mesquite and grass, whose primary function was to provide shade during the day and a little privacy at night.

Those rough houses and the bare footprints back where Janna had been taken told me much of the level of life among the Serona. It was crude and undeveloped, and I didn't have a good feeling about any prisoner they might take. Sometimes, the more primitive the tribe, the more cruelly they would treat and dispatch their prisoners.

Of course, that's not always the case. Some of the poorest groups among the Shoshone, the Diggers, for instance, are the most peaceful—tricky and scheming, but seldom prone to extreme violence. As for the Serona, I could only hope for the best. In the meantime, I would leave nothing to chance.

Men, women, and children, about equal in number, came and went about the village. A surprising number made their way to a house at the edge of the village nearest me, peered into the hut for a time, some even entering, and then wandered away again. I couldn't be absolutely sure, but I had a strong feeling I knew what drew them there. I marked the hut's location well.

One that sat apart, and to the west of the village, was larger. I saw a couple of boys, twelve or so, exit this building. In some tribes, boys live in such houses when the time comes for them to be separated from their mothers. They live in the long house, as it is often called, until they take a wife. I recalled Logan saying that the Serona boys were separated from their mothers at about age nine. Was I looking at their long house? Would that be where young

Christian Dupard was to be found—assuming that he had been taken by Serona, and that he was still alive?

I marked the location of the long house as well, taking particular note of the trees that came to within about fifty feet to the west. I could get fairly close without being seen, if I could think of some way to trick the dogs, or catch the wind just right when it would carry my scent away from the village.

A few small fields bordered the village. Corn grew in some; others appeared to grow vegetables. From the size and height of the plants I guessed they were beans. Beyond the village, near the center of the valley, a herd of horses grazed, numbering about fifty. They looked in good shape, and why wouldn't they be? The valley seemed a very fertile little corner of the world.

I still wondered about water, however. Why would it rain here and not rain a few miles farther back in the valley? That's a technical question I still can't answer, but I recall standing on the edge of the great canyon in the northern part of the Territory and peering down at clouds as they emptied rain into the gorges and great hollows below. I have seen the lightning flash down there, and I have heard the rumble of thunder as clouds I stared down upon turned stormy. Maybe the same thing happened here in this valley.

I counted twenty of the huts. Assigning a man to each hut, which might or might not be the case, and another ten youths to the long house, I came up with possibly a force of thirty I might have to face. Not many, I suppose, but if you are only one and must rescue a prisoner— maybe two—the number tends to grow in your mind.

I kept an eye out for weapons. I saw a few rifles—but mostly, when the men carried a weapon at all, it was a spear or a club. I recalled the tales about the Serona shooting silver bullets and smiled. I doubted that people living in such circumstances and surroundings would have much knowledge of silver, much less the knowledge and skill to pour bullets from it.

I don't know when I became aware of the faint roar. Maybe it was there all along, and I had been too busy surveying the scene below for it to register completely. But suddenly it was there, and it began to intrude more and more. I decided it came from somewhere down the slope from me. Easing myself over the lip of the ledge, I started down. At times the slope was very steep, but I slowed my descent by catching at trees and brush.

The sound grew louder and then turned into a roar— not too loud, but still constant. Then I caught the unmistakable noise of falling water. A few moments later I stood above a cave. A fair-sized stream of water flowed from it and formed a pool before the cave, and then spread into several smaller streams that dribbled down the slope.

This, then, was the sacred water of the Serona—and the cave from which their gods had sent their forebears out into the world. The cave was also supposed to be their source of silver, the existence of which I was beginning to doubt.

An idea was forming in my mind. I wasn't sure it had any merit, but if I decided to give it a try, I needed a safe hiding place close to the village. Most Indians are very superstitious, and tend to steer clear of their sacred places. I couldn't help but wonder how often the Serona visited the cave.

Well, there was only one way to find out.

I circled and came down to the side of the cave. Except for a strip of bank at the edge of the pool, thick grass covered the ground. When the grass where I stepped sprang back into shape, few would be able to tell I had been there. Keeping to the grass, I approached the cave.

The opening was about ten feet high, its width about the same. Using a stone as a stepping place, I went from the grass into the cave without leaving any sign.

There was a dank smell, and a few steps beyond I saw nothing but darkness, but my eyes began to adjust. Soon I made out a narrow ledge. On it was a pile of tinder. That didn't bode well for what I had in mind, but the splinters didn't appear to have been disturbed—not recently, anyway. I took a handful and moved further in. About fifty feet in, I struck a match and stuck it to the tinder. It was dry and laced with tar, and quickly caught fire.

By the light of the torch I examined the cave. I was in a fairly large chamber with a vaulted ceiling, reproducing in echo the murmur of the stream as it moved across the floor. How far back the cave went I had no idea, since the light from my torch fell on nothing but darkness. I took a moment to examine the floor. There was no sign that anyone had ever walked there. In spite of the tinder, I began to think I might have found the place to hide.

Then I hit the toe of my boot on a heavy, very solid rock. My toes stung, and I leaned over to give them a rub. But that rock got my attention. It was a peculiar color— whitish, almost the color of tin. In contrast with the floor of the cave, it was very strange, indeed. I picked it up and was surprised at its weight. This was no ordinary rock. I realized I had seen it before—it was tellurium. I had heard old prospectors tell of finding tellurium that was grainy with gold. I took my knife and scraped into the odd rock. Leaning my torch against the wall of the cave, I placed the ball of tellurium in its light. The yellowish veins gleamed dully up at me. No doubt about it: the weight of the rock came from the heavy deposits of gold.

Tellurium is brittle but nonmetallic. With my knife, I sliced deeply into the ball and found it riddled with gold. I tested two other whitish rocks and found the same thing, and a line of the rocks stretched along the cave's wall as far as my light carried. I was looking at tons of the stuff. Examining the cave wall, I noted the tin-like color there as well. I had no trouble gouging out samples; I found the same telltale streaks of yellow, and the whole wall appeared to be a deposit of tellurium.

My God! I was looking at enough gold to require wagons to haul it away!

And I wasn't the first to test the wall. Others had taken samples out before me, and the cuts were fairly recent.

I suddenly thought of Logan and Farley. Had this gold been the object of the scheme the two had dreamed up? But Farley had said nothing of gold as he was dying. And I had read remorse in his eyes, and in his voice as he spoke.

Could he have died before he had time to mention it? Or maybe he knew nothing about it. Perhaps, Logan had never told him there was gold, but had enlisted Farley's aid merely on the strength of sharing in the $15,000.

Then the real purpose for money dawned on me. The $15,000 was needed to develop the strike. And the Serona? Geraldo Bustamente's men had been recruited to take care of them.

How had Logan learned of the gold? I still can't say for sure, but if I have to guess, I would say he learned of it first from the Serona he hired. He could even have made a trip into the desert to inspect the cave. I recalled then all the tales about silver. Looking at the rocks, I could understand how such tales might have got started. The tellurium might have been mistaken for silver by someone who was ignorant about metals. Maybe Logan first came in looking for silver only to find the gold, instead.

But however he had learned of it, I now knew why he had gone to all the trouble to concoct his Good Samaritan scheme and to follow it through. And Farley? If he hadn't known of the gold, would Logan have shared with him eventually? Or had Logan planned to kill Farley, leaving his remains here in the desert never to be discovered?

More imponderables.

I felt I had discovered enough about the cave. It would serve as a place to hide for a few hours if I decided the plan I had been mulling over was the way to rescue Janna and the boy . . . if the boy indeed was there.

Actually, what I had in mind was to slip into the village at night, get Janna and the boy, find a place to hide nearby, while the Serona rushed off into the desert to chase us. When they were well away, we would make our escape and be long gone by the time they returned. I liked it better and better as I thought about the cave. Of course, if Bustamente's men were to show, they might come straight to the cave, but I had an idea Logan had not told Geraldo Bustamente about the gold. He had promised him a cut of the fifteen thousand, of course, but I felt sure he had never mentioned the gold. With Logan dead, and I was pretty sure he was, the gold might go undiscovered for another hundred years, which suited me fine.

I doused my torch in the stream and started back. I could see fairly well without the flame, since a little light still pushed in from the mouth of the cave. I had to hurry, though, if I were to make it up the slope and to the spring where I had left the moros before darkness fell; climbing the slope in darkness might prove tricky.

When I was about ten feet from the exit of the cave, I caught the sound of voices. I hugged the wall and waited. The two women approached the pool, each carrying a heavy stone jar. They knelt beside the pool, dipped the jars into the pool, and let them fill. When they lifted them out, they stayed a moment to rest and talk.

I stayed where I was, unmoving.

I saw the dog then—a big, mangy, brown cur. He trotted along the bare bank beside the pool and came to the stone I had used as a step. He sniffed it a couple of times. Then he let out a roar and pranced before the cave, his hair on end from his neck to the tip of his tail.

The women gave forth with several shrieks, drowning out the dog. They scrambled down the slippery slope, sliding more than they ran. With each missed step, they let out another shriek. I had a picture in my mind of the whole village streaming up the slope to see what the dog had found in the cave.

I knew I had to face the dog and get out of there. I drew the old Colt to use as a club if he didn't back off and started for him. As I stepped from the cave, he took one look at me and took out after the women. I could only suppose that some of the superstition of the Serona had rubbed off on their dog—that he never expected to see someone looking so different from his masters come at him from the cave.

I then scrambled up the slope to the ledge and sat there a moment in the twilight and watched for them. Remembering the fleeing women, I smiled. They had been young-ish maidens, brown-skinned, with dark hair and eyes, dressed in some kind of brown, rough cloth. I wondered if I might not have just become the central character in the next legend to be passed down among the Serona by those two young women—the night the gods appeared to them, or at least to their dog, in the sacred cave.

The moros was still working at the grass when I reached the spring. She threw her head up and glanced at me, the look suggesting that I should be stoking up on a little food myself. I decided she was right.

A little light still penetrated the trees. I found a couple of rocks the proper size and set off along the ledge. I didn't go far before a grouse scooted from underfoot. I made the kill with my first throw.

I wasn't concerned about the Serona smelling the smoke from a fire. They had too many of their own fires below, scenting up the valley, for them to notice one more. The light was another matter. I needed a place that couldn't be seen from below.

I found a broad cutout that ran back into the slope. The place was overgrown with brush, but I pushed through. At the back I cleared enough space to lay my fire, using the limbs I broke away as fuel. I skinned the bird as the fire burned to hot ash. While the grouse roasted, I went back for the mare. She had filled her belly by then and stood, her head down, taking a well-deserved rest.

I offered her more water, which she refused. Then I led her deep into the cutout where I stripped her of gear and rubbed her down with grass. I hoped my efforts communicated to her just how indispensable she was to me.

By the time I finished, the bird was done. I ate it as I sat over the bed of red coals. Then I spread my bedroll and crawled into it. I hadn't slept well in several nights, and if I slipped into the village later on, I badly needed to get some rest now.

I dozed off to the sounds of the moros who nibbled at the brush around her from time to time.

CHAPTER 14

I HAD the feeling I might have overslept when I woke up. I checked the stars. They looked about right. I crawled out of my bedroll.

I guess I wouldn't have been too disappointed if I had overslept. I was tired, the moros was tired. We still had a long run to make even if I was able to free Janna and the boy. A day spent lying up in the cutout would have put us in a little better shape to make the run. On the other hand, some curious Serona might decide to explore the slope after the women spread their story of what happened at the cave.

I ate what remained of the grouse, packed my gear, and saddled the moros. Rather than risk a spill, I decided to walk down the slope leading the mare. She didn't take to entering the cave. I had to coax her in.

God, it was dark in there, but I didn't light a torch. Remembering the layout, I eased along, one hand extended, the other holding the mare's rein, and I tested each step before I put a foot down. I knew when I came to the tellurium rocks, but I didn't stop until I was well beyond. I put a couple of the heavier rocks on the end of the mare's rein to weight it down. She was well trained. She would be there when I returned, and I suspect no horse was ever tethered more expensively.

I was relieved to be outside again. By contrast the night seemed dangerously bright. Beyond the trees the valley seemed even brighter, but I was committed.

147

Remembering how slippery the slope beneath the cave had been when the women fled, I made a wide circle to stay on dry land. Still, the slope was thickly covered, and I had to move slowly. I kept thinking of the dogs. Even the rustle of a few leaves might be picked up by them.

Finally I reached level ground, and through the trees I saw the dark outline of the first hut—Janna's hut, if I had surmised correctly. I sat there a moment and studied the space separating the trees and the hut. There was maybe fifty yards with no sign of cover. A late, pale quarter-moon still threw far too much light on that open stretch.

The possibility of attracting the attention of a village dog was increased tenfold now. And I had no idea of the habits of the Serona men. Did they post night guards? Or if they didn't ordinarily, might not the appearance of Janna so near the village cause them now to exercise such caution?

I engaged in a wordless prayer for wind—enough to rattle the leaves a little, covering any sound I might make, even if it did not come from a direction that would carry my scent away from the village and some keen-nosed dog. My attitude of supplication did not pay off. Not a breath of wind stirred.

A few night insects were making some noise, but they were no help. Rather, they made me even more nervous. If you know how to read night sounds—and no one is more skilled in this than the Indians I have known, insects at night give the reverse of a noisy alarm—but an alarm, all the same. There is a moving pocket of silence about anything that moves at night. The insects, all of them, cut their sounds the instant they detect movement. When it passes on, they start up again. For someone hearing the change, that silent interlude translates into "night prowler." Fortunately, insects don't differentiate between men and beasts. At last I made the shadow at the rear of the hut, and I was still undetected.

Suddenly, from a hut on the opposite side of the circle of houses, a dog cut loose. I forced myself to crouch low and remain there despite the dog. Other dogs picked up the chorus. I drew the old Colt, positive the time had come when I would be forced to make a stand.

I caught the sound of approaching movement in the grass. It came from the direction of the barking dog, but he didn't sound as if he had moved closer. What then? Another dog? A silent one? The movement seemed slow for a dog. Then a giant armadillo passed between me and the next hut. A moment later the village was quiet again.

There was no opening in that end of the hut—neither door nor window, just finger-wide cracks between the limbs of which the hut had been constructed, however. I put an ear to one of these and heard the sound of breathing. They were sleep-spaced breaths; whether they were being made by Janna remained to be seen.

I began a slow, cautious circle around the hut, putting each foot down carefully. Everything depended on me not alerting the dogs, or a guard, who might be in position before the hut. I made the front corner and peered around it. I didn't see anything. The guard, if there was one, was inside. I also had the nervous thought that maybe Janna wasn't in the hut at all. I might be about to intrude on a family of sleeping Serona.

I stood by the doorway, over which was hung a rough cloth, and pondered what to do. Moonlight struck the front of the hut, clearly outlining me against it. Every moment I lingered increased the risk of my being seen—either by dog or man. I had to make up my mind.

Thinking of the time and effort spent in getting so close, I lifted the cloth and stepped inside.

I was relieved when my foot set down on dirt floor. Anything else might have produced a sound. I had to adjust my eyes to the darkness of the hut, and I stepped to the side of the doorway until that happened. Finally, the darkness began to fade and I could examine what was around me.

There was little other than one sleeper who lay along the rear wall at about the point where I had stood outside. But if that was Janna, there was no guard. I found that a little strange until I asked myself where a prisoner might go without a horse, and I would have bet almost anything the horses were guarded.

I still held the Colt in my hand. I kept it there, prepared to use it as a club if the sleeper turned out to be anyone other than Janna. I cautiously eased across the hut and knelt by the sleeper. I recognized her before I saw her features. Drifting up from the blankets was the unmistakable, faint odor of the perfume I had come to associate with her—like the faint smell of spring flowers, though too indistinct to identify the blossom.

But I could see her face. Even in sleep, and with her eyes closed, she seemed to show concern. I fought the urge to lean even closer to her face—maybe to steal a kiss there in the darkness. The thought sent a strange guilty thrill through me. But I was so close, and my mind had been filled with thoughts of her for days. I thought for a moment of what was happening to me—how futile it was for someone like me to fall in love with a woman like Janna Dupard. I figured those silent thoughts were as close as I would ever come to confessing my feelings—as close as I dared to come. After all, this was Janna Dupard of St.

Louis, wealthy heiress. As for me, never had I felt more like a desert rat.

I put a hand over her mouth and shook her gently. She came awake fighting.

"Janna! It's me! Sax! Stop it!"

She stopped so suddenly, was so still I thought she might have fainted.

"At last," she finally whispered. "I knew you'd come."

"We've got to get out of here," I whispered.

She caught my shirt in a firm hold.

"No. We can't leave yet. I saw him."

Even after she said it, I still found it a little hard to believe, although I had, of course, shared her hopes. But even after what Farley had said to me, I still had doubts.

"You *did* see him?" I asked.

"Yes."

"Did you talk with him?"

"No. There was no chance."

"Did he recognize you?"

"I . . . I think so, but I'm not sure."

I wasn't prepared for that. Christian had been six when he was captured. Only three years had passed since he had seen his mother. Surely, he would still know her. There seemed only two explanations if he didn't. The boy wasn't Christian or something traumatic had wiped the past from the boy's mind.

"I don't mean we'll leave the valley without him," I told her. "But we can't stay here. I have a plan. We'll talk about it outside."

She seemed a bit skeptical, but she came.

I didn't stop until we were among the trees at the foot of the slope. We sat on a boulder in their shadows and looked at each other for a moment.

She asked about Levi. I found it impossible to explain where he was just then. I was still having trouble accepting it, and the words just weren't there for me to speak of his betrayal.

"I'll explain later," I said. "Right now we have to think about Christian. Are you sure the boy is your son?"

"What do you mean? Of course, I'm sure!" she answered hotly.

"Then why didn't he recognize you? It's been only three years. He would surely remember you."

"I know," she said. "I can only explain it one way."

"How?"

"Maybe he's afraid that if he lets the Serona know who I am, they'll take some sort of action to protect him from me—maybe do something to me."

I had to accept that as a possibility, of course. But I still leaned toward the theory that the boy she had seen was not Christian. I knew how much she wanted to find the boy. What mother wouldn't grasp at any straw?

"Are you absolutely sure he's Christian?" I asked.

I expected her to flare up again, but she didn't.

"Give me some credit," she said quietly but firmly. "In the first place, it is obvious this boy is no Indian. He has brown hair, and its shade is the exact shade of every Dupard man I've known. He has the Dupard eyes and nose as well. I couldn't be mistaken. I give you my word he is Christian."

I had to be satisfied with that.

"Did you notice anything that made you think he might know you but was obviously holding back from you?" I asked.

"I caught him staring at me several times. He looked frightened. I was expecting him to come to the hut when everyone was asleep. In fact, I thought you were Christian when I woke up. We have to get him out of here, Sax," she continued. "Tell me about your plan."

"Do you remember the large hut just to the west of the village?" I began.

"Yes."

"I think the boys are housed there. Do you know it that's true?"

"I've seen them coming and going from there," she answered.

"Well, here's the plan. I'm going to start a commotion on the opposite side of the village. I want you to wait near that hut until the noise begins. The boys will come flying out—I hope. Somehow you've got to get the boy's attention. Don't let him follow the others."

"How?" she asked.

"I don't know. Tackle him. Club him, but stop him."

"All right, I'll find a way."

"That will be the riskiest moment. If he doesn't remember you, he'll fight. He'll spread the alarm. If they catch you, they'll put a guard on you. I might not be able to make contact with you again. So you have to keep that from happening if you can."

"I will," she said.

I had known all along she had nerve. I hadn't been prepared for her to exhibit so much, but I was grateful. No other woman I had ever known would have accepted such formidable challenge so coolly.

"What next?" she asked.

"Do you remember the cave the priest wrote about?"

"Yes."

"It's up this slope and a little to the west of where we are now. Get to the cave as fast as you can. You'll find my mare back there, so don't be frightened if you bump into her."

"We can't all three ride one horse," she said.

"I intend to get more—when I cut that herd loose and stampede them through the village."

"When do we start?" she asked.

"No time like now," I said, looking at the sky.

The moon had faded, and the stars had begun to withdraw. I figured we had maybe another hour before daybreak. That should give me plenty of time to scout the herd, and hopefully, take care of any guard.

I stood up. She did the same. I felt her hand take mine. I waited for her to speak, but she didn't, but just stood there with my hand in hers.

It seemed an invitation, and I couldn't resist. I slipped a hand behind her back and held her against me. Her body, firm but feminine, pressed against me. Her face was turned up to mine. The light was faint, but I looked into dark, luminous eyes. They drew my head down like a magnet.

I found her lips, and I expected her to resist. She didn't. Instead, she kissed me back, her lips searching as hungrily as mine. I suddenly had the sensation my world was tilting—about to tumble upside down. I broke the kiss, dropped my hands to my side, and stepped back.

"I'm . . . I'm sorry," I managed.

"What for?" she asked. "I wanted that as badly as you. You knew that, didn't you?"

"No, I . . ."

The implications seemed more than we had time to handle just then.

"We have to get going," I said firmly.

"All right—for now," she answered.

She went west. I stood and watched her fade into the darkness. There was the chance I would never see her again. I turned east, trying to damper down the wild feelings that threatened to explode inside me—trying to calm down before I made a mistake that would wake the whole village.

CHAPTER 15

I CONTINUED east until I was well beyond the village. I could hear an occasional snort from the horse herd. I went well past before I turned into the valley. I wanted to approach the herd on the side away from the huts. They were bunched very close together, and when I came near, I found them penned in a waist-high rope held up by temporary pegs to form a makeshift corral. The animals had room to stir about a little, but they couldn't roam. Apparently, they were trained not to test the rope, for a simple push would have sent it over. They shied away a few steps as I approached. I turned into a stone and allowed them to settle down.

Moving slowly, I followed the rope until I spotted the guard. He sat on a stone, his profile to me. His head slumped forward a little as if dozing. I had the old Colt in my hand. Step by slow step, I came up. When I raised the Colt, he seemed to sense his danger even in sleep. He came awake, turned toward me, and I saw his eyes for a moment. I brought the butt of the gun down hard. He crumpled.

I checked him, and he was out cold.

I circled the heard searching for a second guard, but there wasn't any. Coming back to the rock, I knelt to see how the Serona was faring. He was beginning to stir. I hated to do it, but I felt I had no other choice. I hit him again. I pulled him close to the rock so he wouldn't be trampled. That good deed paid a return. Beside the rock

I found a pile of halters—rough headstalls in widespread use among some tribes. I selected two, went quickly to the herd, and slipped beneath the rope.

The horses had become accustomed to me somewhat by then, but I still made them nervous. The animal I had my eyes on faded away, as did the second and the third, leaving an open path before me whichever way I turned. I had the feeling they would spook at any sudden move, and I knew the rope wouldn't hold them. Frustrated, I stood there and tried to think of a way to coax one into accepting me and the halter.

Fate came down on my side again. I spotted Janna's mare. Crooning a few words at her, I approached. She seemed to recognize me, and I slipped her nose into the halter, and then over her ears. I gave her a couple of love pats and swung up. I had picked her for her gentleness, and she didn't buck. Easing her alongside a pony, I had the halter on him before he realized I was on the mare's back.

I didn't look for saddles. If the rest of the plan was successful, we'd ride bareback out of the desert.

I stayed astride the mare as I reached down to put my knife to the rope. I cut through it and gave it a jerk. The rope toppled, and I crowded the horses, sending them straight for the huts. I wanted to create as much confusion as possible around the village, and stampeding horses, especially at night, would do that. To inspire them a little, I fired a couple of shots into the air. They flattened out and began to run, but they headed into the center of the valley away from village. I sent the mare alongside and turned them. Then I wheeled her about and rode east. At the proper time I intended to cut into the trees along the slope and work my way back to the cave.

A strange thing happened then—maybe because the horses were nervous about a headlong dash toward the village. At least half of them veered away and turned back toward me. I guess they caught sight of the mare I was on and the Serona pony. At any rate, they made a beeline in my direction.

That suited me fine. If the Serona thought someone was making off with half of their herd, they would give chase twice as fast.

The explosions from the Colt had stirred the village up even before the horses hit. I heard shouts and squeals. Someone fired a rifle—probably at a shadow. Meanwhile, that portion of the herd that was following me was now on my heels. I could feel their breath on my back when I made a cut. They shot past me, the pounding of their hoofs echoing up the tree-studded slope, and gradually fading down the canyon. I turned back west and worked my way up to the shoulder.

I kept to the shoulder until I heard the sound of water from below. I pulled up and slid to the ground. I still wasn't willing to trust a mount down that steep slope with me astride. I felt doubly nervous about it without a saddle.

I think the Indian pony might have balked at entering the cave, but the mare set a good example. I led them back several yards and stopped, listening for some sound which would indicate that Janna and, hopefully, the boy had reached there ahead of me. The only thing I heard was the moros—a stamp and a friendly snort as she caught my smell and that of the other horses.

I didn't like it. At least half an hour had passed since I had fired that first shot that had awakened the village. That seemed to me to be plenty of time for Janna to make it to the cave if she had managed to corral the boy. If she hadn't—if she hadn't got to him—I knew she wouldn't come. She would remain down there and fight for him, even fight the boy if it came to that.

Easing the two horses along, I moved back to where the moros was tethered. I tied their reins to hers, hoping she would keep them there while I went back outside for a look.

The ongoing commotion in the village was getting even louder. A few fires had been started up. Through the trees I saw Serona grouped about the fires gesturing angrily. I gathered they had missed their horses. Then several mounted riders swept through the village and headed east. I was surprised they had taken so long to round up mounts, but my plan was working. I figured there were at least twenty riders, which would be most of the men, if my estimates were on target.

I stood beside the small pool and checked the slope below. Anyone making the climb just now would have to be Janna. There was nothing. Not even a leaf stirred.

I started down the slope. With most of the men away maybe I could get her out—at least find out what happened to her. I guess I forgot where I was, and I was moving pretty fast as well. Suddenly, my feet went out from under me. My butt hit the ground, and I began to slide. I skidded about ten feet on soapstone, the slickest surface on earth, before I could grab a bush. Finally, I hit one and wrapped myself around it. Lying there, I didn't know whether to laugh or cuss.

I didn't have time for either. I heard a noise from below and had to scramble across that slick mess to throw myself into the shade of a thicket. My God! What a predicament! That bank was as slick as grease, and I might have to face the Serona while I was clinging to it!

I took out the old Colt and got ready.

I caught the sound of voices, and they got louder. Then I saw their outline between me and the fires below. One medium sized, the other smaller. Janna and the boy? I huddled in the shadow of the thicket, afraid to believe it. How could something which, a moment ago, had seemed such a catastrophe turn out well?

I recognized Janna's voice, though. She was urging the boy along, which I thought was curious, since the boy was in the lead and pulling her along. They were working their way up the shallow stream to hide their sign.

"Are you all right?" I asked stepping from the shadows.

They were both startled, but Janna recognized my voice immediately. The boy was a different matter. He came at me like a shot. My footing was fragile even without having to withstand a charge. When he hit me, I went down again, catching the same bush which had stopped my slide before.

He landed on top of me, a flurry of flying fists and feet. The only thing I could do was squeeze him to me, which I tried to do without hurting him, but he was a little fighting wildcat and hard to pin down.

The next instant Janna was over us. She grabbed the boy.

"Christian!" she whispered fiercely. "Stop it! Stop it at once!"

I let go. She didn't have all that much size, but she held him above me, talking to him all the while. Finally, the boy was still.

"Are you all right?" she asked me.

"Half skinned from being clawed, but other than that . . ."

"I had told him you would be in the cave. When you jumped out like that, you frightened us."

"Jumped out!" I sputtered. "I . . ." But I let it go.

The boy stood beside her. Dawn had begun to creep into the trees, providing enough light for me to see him. He was a curious-looking little fellow with long, fine-textured, brown hair that reached to his shoulders. A band about his forehead held it close. He was dressed in something akin to the brown skirt worn by the two women I had seen, except his was shorter. He was a tough-looking little fellow, and there was a defiant look on his face as he looked me over.

"Christian, this is Mr. Younger," Janna said. "We owe him a lot, you and I. I wouldn't be here without him."

He didn't warm up. I offered him a hand which he refused. Janna gave me a look which asked for under-standing.

"Get him into the cave while I get rid of the signs of our scuffle," I said. "Stay in the stream. You had a good idea there."

"It was Christian's idea," she said.

They moved away up the stream, taking their time, which was the only way to do it. I stood in the stream and sloshed water on the bank until the marks were washed away.

They were waiting for me in the pool. We waded through. Just inside the cave we took to the bank. Looking back, I saw the first streaks of sunlight break through the trees from the east.

Sitting in the back of the cave without knowing what was happening wasn't easy. The darkness didn't help matters, either. The only thing to focus the eyes on was the round hole of light, which was the entrance to the cave. We sat there and stared at that mostly.

We were silent in the beginning, but Janna asked if we would be overheard if we talked. I didn't think so. The water made a smooth, steady sound, and we were well back in the cave.

She talked with the boy mostly. I think she was trying to get him over his initial shyness. When he responded, his English was slow and hesitant, as though he didn't find the words easily. Often he resorted to Spanish. I understood only a little, but Janna, apparently, was fluent. Gradually, however, she led him back into English.

She asked about his family among the Serona. He told her a little of Toucan, the man who, apparently, had raised him. But mostly he spoke of Brown Leaf, the woman who had been his mother. Janna pounced eagerly on every detail, as if she needed to know every aspect of his life away from her. I found the description of Serona life much like that of any other Indian tribe.

I think for some time she had been leading up to the stagecoach raid. When she did ask him about it, he lapsed into silence. She prodded him. When he answered, it was in very excited Spanish. For once, Janna let him talk in Spanish. When he was finished, she turned to me.

"Did you understand any of it?" she asked.

"Hardly any."

"The Serona didn't make the raid."

"Who was it then?"

"Apaches."

That didn't surprise me. I had had trouble believing the Serona had raided that far north before I knew much about them. Having come to know something of them, the idea of such a raid had seemed even more unlikely.

"How did he wind up with the Serona?" I asked.

"They traded for him—traded a horse."

She stopped talking, obviously thinking of that. I didn't know whether the idea of young Christian being swapped for a horse made her angry or what. I figured both she and the boy were lucky, however. I doubted the boy would have survived the hard life of an Apache. Without the trade, she might never have seen him again.

But she wasn't angry. After a moment, she said, "And to think all this time I have blamed the Serona—hated them. As it turns out, they probably saved him for me. I have to think of some way to repay them."

That thought intrigued me. What could a woman living in St. Louis do for a very small tribe of Indians living deep in Mexico?

I still had told her nothing of Logan and Farley's betrayal. I decided the time had come to do it.

"Do you remember the two men who held back when Bustamente's men had us cornered on the ridge?" I asked.

"Yes."

"I found out who they were."

"And?"

"One was Logan. The other was Richard Farley."

She got very quiet. When she didn't speak, I reached out a hand to her shoulder. She was rigid, but after a moment she began to relax.

"Are you certain? Did you see them up close?" she asked.

"Close enough," I said. "I fought with Farley. He pulled a little derringer on me."

"I've seen that gun," she said.

"I had lost my own gun, but I got him with a throw of my knife. That's how he died."

I didn't supply any more details, but I wanted her to know he had not had an easy death.

"Did you get a chance to speak with him?" she asked.

"Yes, he mentioned you. I think he had a lot of guilt."

"Did he . . . Did he say what possessed him to do such a thing?"

"He mentioned gambling debts . . . some bad business ventures. He gave those as his reasons."

"And Logan? Is he dead?"

"I'm not absolutely sure. He was hit. The last I saw of him he was running across the sand. He fell in the fire when he was shot. His clothes caught. He was burning."

"Now tell me about Levi. I know something awful happened to him. I keep thinking of his wife . . . how she's going to hurt."

I knew I had to tell her, but I didn't find it easy.

"He wasn't killed," I said.

"Then what happened to him?" she asked, obviously puzzled.

"He ran off with the money during the fight," I said.

"You mean you found it?"

"Yes. I saw you come from those rocks. I remembered you didn't have the bag when I helped you mount. I figured you had left it in the rocks. My God, how I wish I hadn't found it. Levi would be here with us now. I wouldn't have to repeat all of this to Amanda."

The boy had listened in silence to all of this. I wondered what it meant to him. Did he understand such betrayal? I doubted he did. He had been too young to understand the importance of such values, and I had no idea of what he had been taught of such things by the Serona.

"I'm sorry," Janna said. "The two of you were such friends. Now that's gone, and it's a terrible waste. There has to be something to explain it which we don't know about."

I didn't explain about the transfer. I didn't think it justified such an act.

"I have been thinking about Amanda," she said. "Why tell her about the theft. Why not say he was killed in the fight. I don't care about the money. Anyway, it was to help me get Christian back." She put an arm about him and held him against her. "I have him now. That's all that's important to me."

"What if Levi were to send for her?" I asked.

"If he does, let him explain things to her. I would like to hear what he would say to that good woman. I can't imagine the words myself."

I was running that through my mind when I heard the sound of shots. They were distant, their sound barely audible above the noise of the water. They grew steadily louder, and they came from the east along the canyon. There were two distinct sets of explosions, one closer in, the other further away down the canyon. Those more distant had the rhythm of repeater rifles. Was someone attacking the Serona?

Without a word the boy was suddenly up and running.

"Christian!" Janna shouted as she chased after him.

I ran after them until I was halfway to the cave's mouth. I turned back then. The battle down below had suddenly heated up. I was remembering Geraldo Bustamente's heavily armed men. I figured they had followed me into the valley. I couldn't stand by while they slaughtered the Serona, and I couldn't go down there on foot. I needed the moros.

When I reached her, I scrambled up, unable to find the stirrup in the darkness. I'd forgotten, too, that the reins of the other horses were still tied to hers. She pulled them around when I turned her.

I gave her her head, trusting her to get through the darkness of the cave. Between me and the opening, I saw the running silhouettes of Janna and the boy against the sunlight. They made it outside just before me. I stopped long enough to give them mounts.

The boy scrambled up.

I reached out and grabbed him. "You stay with your mother!" I shouted. "Look after her! I'll go down and give them a hand!"

I had no idea what he would do. Apparently, young Christian felt great loyalty to the Serona. I took some unwarranted pride in that as I sent the moros skidding down the slope, and below me panic had broken out in the village.

Just then the first rays of the morning sun hit the valley.

CHAPTER 16

I WASN'T certain Janna could hold young Christian back. The thought that the Serona were under attack had made him wild.

I came off the slope just east of the village and pulled up beneath the last fringe of trees. The fight was in progress just before me. The Serona, in a line across the valley, were being forced into a slow retreat. Their losses didn't appear too heavy yet, but I saw bodies and a few loose horses. But unless they turned the tide, the women and children in the village would be at risk soon.

I couldn't miss the leaders of the attackers. They were led by Geraldo Bustamente, his heavyset, paunchy figure giving his mount a swayback look. Beside him was Logan, who had, after all, escaped my bullet as well as the flames.

Then I learned just how far back the devious, diabolical plan went. Flanking Bustamente and Logan were the final two of the trio who had attempted to waylay me in the Grand Wash country—Ferret Face Skittles and the dudish looking Lawson. I was glad to see them there. It was a score that needed settling. There were others there as well who didn't appear to be members of Bustamente's bandit gang—brought in, no doubt, from north of the border to help out.

They faced the fading Serona, but they weren't charging. They were more methodical, moving slowly, laying down a barrage that took more and more of the Indians out of action. There was no time for a count, but I estimated at least twenty in the line as they pushed slowly but surely toward the village. Within minutes they would reach the huts unless something unforeseen happened.

I guess the Serona thought the same. I saw women and children being hustled out of the village and across the open space and into the trees on the slope where, hopefully, Janna and Christian waited for me.

The scene was much like that of other battles, though this one might be on a smaller scale. The sun was climbing fast now. Its rays beat down, filling the valley with ovenlike heat that pushed up and into my face even in the shade of the trees. The boom of exploding rifles was constant. The sounds were extended when they hit the trees on the slope and were thrown back into and across the valley. Overhead puffs of smoke from exploding powder formed miniature clouds as they drifted west before a slow wind and dispersed. Beneath those, more tightly knit puffs, more recently exploded, hung together until they reached the level of the wind. Beneath was the battle line, and the Indians were slowly being pushed back—almost, now, up against the first hut.

Ordinarily, I like to give a fellow warning before I start shooting at him. I decided an exception was in order here. The use of surprise seemed justified, since, as soon as I took a hand, at least half of those rifles would be turned on me.

I wheeled the moros back into the trees to protect her. Grabbing the Winchester from its boot, I returned, dropped to one knee to steady my aim, and drew a bead. I wanted the riders who led the deadly march—the ones at the point—Bustamente, Logan, Skittles, and Lawson. With them out of the way the Serona might be able to turn the tide, since some of the confidence of the others would be deflated.

Skittles was first, partially blocking Bustamente, who was next, from view. My first bullet slammed into him. He was a lightweight in every respect. My lead not only knocked him from the saddle, but threw him directly into the path of Bustamente's horse. Skittles's own mount, spooked, took off toward the village, while Bustamente's bowed up and began to pitch. For the moment, Bustamente was kept busy trying to calm his mount.

That horse, the same black stallion, seemed inspired, however. Maybe he was just tired of his heavy load. Whatever the cause, he bucked stronger the more Bustamente tried to bring him under control. I took a shot at him anyway. I missed, but Logan was just beyond him. My bullet ripped into him, but the shot wasn't fatal. Logan held on. The man had more lives than a cat.

He was the first to take note of where the shots came from. Staring in my direction, I think he recognized me. He sent his own horse into the shoulder of Bustamente's mount, throwing the animal off stride and helping to bring him under control. Then he shouted something to Bustamente and pointed toward me.

Bustamente must have recognized me then. He swung his tired horse in a tight circle and sent him toward me, yelling at his men as he passed them, who fell in behind him. He was followed by both Logan and Lawson as well. I had a dozen men, at least, coming at me, and coming fast.

I worked the rifle as fast as I could. I no longer took aim at men, but at their mounts. I had to thin their numbers even if I didn't turn the charge. Horses stumbled and went down. I saw two men scramble up from broadsided mounts that were still kicking. At least one, I think it was Lawson, was pinned beneath his mount. I heard him scream, and a terrible thing it was—louder than the explosions that broke and rolled along the valley, a final exclamation of what it is like to die on a battlefield.

Bustamente and Logan led the charge against me. They were bearing down on me from no more than fifty yards, but even so I saw something to my right that gave me heart. My distraction had taken some of the pressure off the Serona. They had now turned and were working their way back into the valley, the charge on the village broken.

I took heart at the sight, but I wasn't sure the turnabout had come in time to help me, for neither Logan nor Bustamente seemed to be aware of what was happening behind them. They seemed intent only on one thing: getting to me, as if I were the only one who stood between them and getting to whatever had brought them into the desert—the gold, presumably.

Or maybe it was more than that. Maybe by now they thought they had a personal score to settle with me. I had escaped their loop so long: once in the Grand Wash country, once in the saloon in Yuma, and on the ridge in the desert. All that effort and yet to have failed. That must have nettled them some.

I slowed my fire now, concentrating on Logan and Bustamente. I wasn't trying now for their horses. I wanted to put a bullet into them, knowing that if I took the leaders out, the others would have no heart to continue the fight.

My rifle clicked on empty.

There was no time to reload. I took out the old Colt. Six chances to down them before the Colt was empty. There were four of them, and they were still a little beyond the accurate range of the old gun. I did a very hard thing. I held my fire as they bore down on me.

I could see their faces, and Bustamente, at least, knew what had happened. He wore a triumphant sneer, and he spurred his mount to greater speed, coming directly at me. I lifted the Colt, took aim—and waited. I didn't have a chance to squeeze the trigger, however. A rifle exploded from just behind me. I whirled, afraid one of the bandits had slipped up behind me, or worse still, Janna had decided to come to my aid and would now have to face Bustamente and Logan.

My astonishment was complete. It was Levi. He was still mounted, and he was pumping shots into the charging horsemen.

"Don't just stand there gaping, son!" he yelled at me. "Take care of Bustamente! I didn't kill him! I just got his horse!"

He spurred his mount past me and sent him at Logan. Logan suddenly wheeled his own mount around and fled across the valley. Levi was at his heels.

Levi was right about Bustamente. His horse was down, but the big bandit was dragging himself up when I turned back. He had lost his rifle, but his six-gun was still in its holster. He grabbed for it and turned to face me.

We were within twenty feet of each other, guns drawn and trained on each other. Something, probably the knowledge that we could kill each other, held us suspended.

Behind Bustamente I saw Levi take Logan out with a shot to his back. Further on, the Mexicans had turned tail. The Indians were swarming after them, taking them down one by one. The valley was littered with bodies now. Stray horses swarmed back and forth.

Bustamente might not be looking at all of that, but he must have been aware of what was happening. His eyes were pinned on me. They had a crafty look, as if he might have come up with one last scheme.

We stood there, guns drawn, mine aimed at him, his at me. Odd that we both seemed reluctant to shoot, since there was death all about us, and more being dealt to his bandits out there in the valley. But those deaths had to do with other men, nothing to do with Geraldo Bustamente—at this moment.

"I hear all the time how fast you are with the draw, Señor Younger," he said in his thick Spanish accent. "Señor Skittles, he speak of it. And Lawson. They say how you beat Horse Neck—how your hand was but a flash. I laugh. I say no man is so fast—no man but Geraldo Bustamente! I, señor, am the fastest gun north and south of the border. I prove it to you now."

I wasn't sure what he was up to. How would a shootout serve him now? Even if he outdrew me, he wouldn't get out of the valley alive. Already the Serona had begun to celebrate their victory out there in the valley. And there was Levi. Bustamente would have to kill him to leave the valley.

But he stood no chance as it was. Neither of us would get a shot off before the other shot as well. As close as we were, we would both die. That being the case, I couldn't fare much worse whatever he had in mind.

"What do you want?" I asked. "A shootout?"

"Why not?" he asked. You might beat me. If you do, you live. Skittles, he make a bet with me. He say you faster. You let me find out, eh?"

"What purpose will it serve, Bustamente? You and your men are whipped. Skittles is dead. Even if you beat me, you will die. Give it up. Drop your gun."

But I knew what possessed him. The same thing was tugging at my insides. The man who lives by the gun is a vain creature. He wants that flush of pride when he knows he has proven once again he is best. And it's more than pride—a certain savagery that the best of men sometimes have to struggle with. I struggled then, tried to choke it down, but it was there in me just as surely as it was in Bustamente. A gunman needs it—like a drug—even if he dies the next minute. That's the way it is . . . the way it will always be.

The fighting had now stopped. The valley was silent. The smell of spent powder hung in the air.

"I will die either way," Bustamente said, "but if I kill you, they will talk. Geraldo Bustamente will be the legend! Bandits will tell of me as long as there are bandits. They will tell this story around campfires for a hundred years!"

He was right, of course. That's the way legends are born. But what if I beat him? And I thought of something else. Did he know of the gold? Had Logan, now dead, taken the big bandit into his confidence? I had my doubts, but I didn't want to take any chances. I didn't want word of the gold to spread. The Serona deserved a chance to live in peace. Someone would come along and discover the gold again someday. But for now, the Serona would be saved. I had to kill Bustamente.

I wish I could say that was my sole reason. But inside me there was something else. Something ugly. Something Levi had always known. Something Janna Dupard had sensed, even if she had offered me that apology. I actually wanted this fight. Later, I would feel shame and guilt . . . if I lived. But just then, the challenge was the thing.

"All right, Bustamente, holster your gun."

"And you, Señor Younger? You will holster yours?"

"Yes."

"What the hell are you up to, Sax?" Levi asked then.

He sat his horse to my right. Behind him the Serona

had gathered—even the women had returned. In their front I saw Janna. The boy was beside her. Her arm was around his shoulders.

"He wants a shootout, Levi," I said. "I've decided to oblige him."

"Don't be a damned fool, Sax!" Levi said. "I've got my gun on him. I'll kill the bastard myself if he pulls that trigger."

"Stay out of it, Levi. This is between me and him."

I heard Levi swear. I took a final quick look at Janna. She had a look of horror and disbelief on her face. She seemed suddenly to class both me and Bustamente in the same category—both of us gunslingers and killers, the thrill of the face-off more important to us than anything else. I almost backed down in the face of the judgment she was passing on me, but there was the gold—the fate of the Serona. And there was the surge of that shameful thrill in my chest.

Bustamente looked nervous. There had been a sheen of sweat on his face all along. Now the droplets rolled down his fat cheeks and jowls, his forehead was beaded. The burning sun, maybe his own nerves, seemed to squeeze and suck the moisture from him.

The crafty look was gone from his eyes now. There was something else there, however—whatever it is that drives men at such a moment—the vanity, the false dream of glory, his desire that others remember this act. And there was fear. There is always fear. And the knowledge of being near death—from my gun or Levi's.

"Anytime, Bustamente," I said, trying to ignore some of those same feelings in myself.

In a showdown you learn to read another's eyes—that is, if you survive a few times. There is that instant in which the message, on its way to the hand, is flashed in the eye. That is the cue. Strike then and quickly—and shoot straight. That is the way to survive in this business.

I read the message and made a stab for my gun. We drew at the same instant, and there were two explosions as one.

Dynamite exploded in my side. I fought to stay up—get off another shot if I had to.

Bustamente was grabbing for his chest. He seemed to be fighting something inside him—something deep within his flesh, which had entered just at that point. He scratched wildly, digging his fingers into the crimson tide that flooded his chest.

He went down then, and I saw his face. Death marked it with the look of defeat. He would never know how nearly his bullet had come to fatally marking me—that he had come within an inch of the glory he sought.

I knew, and it made no difference. He was down, and I was up. And I had beat him—maybe the fastest gun I had ever faced.

Levi rushed to me then. "Goddammit, boy! Will you never learn?"

"And you, Levi? Did you learn? Did you come back with the money?"

"Yes, you damn fool! I lost my head, and I'll pay the price. As will you."

"What do you mean?"

"There," he said.

His nod was toward where Janna and the boy had stood. I turned and looked there. They were gone. A few of the Serona still stood around. They gazed on me with curious, strange eyes.

"Where are you hit, Sax?" Levi asked.

His question was needless. My bloodsoaked shirt identified the spot. He ripped the shirt away and took a look. He poked around in the wound a moment.

"Went through cleanly," he said. "We'll clean it up. A few days' rest and you'll be good as new."

But I knew better. I would always see the look on Janna Dupard's face just before I drew on Geraldo Bustamente. And I already felt the loss, because she knew now she had been right all along. There was something about me—something that made me a lot like Bustamente. Oh, not completely. Just something I had never tamed. Something I might never tame.

Levi led me to a rock nearby. I sat down. He wrapped my wound in my shirt.

"That's just temporary," he said. "Just until I can get you to water."

"Why did you come back, Levi?" I asked.

"I . . . I couldn't not come back. I kept seeing you down there in that sandbed fighting for your life. That bag got heavier with every step. And I kept seeing Amanda's face when you told her what I had done. I turned back then."

"Well, thank God you did. You saved my skin again. Levi, about the money. I don't think you have anything to fear. Janna is too happy to have the boy back. Your showing up in the nick of time made all the difference. I expect she'll hand that bag of money over to you, or the equivalent once you're home again."

"No, I'm going to take my medicine. I'll resign my commission when I get back. I'll tell Amanda. That will be the worst. Telling her I stole, and that I let you down, Sax."

"Tell Amanda if you want, but this won't make any difference in the way she feels about you. Resign your commission, but don't bring up the money. Stay out here,

Levi. This is where you belong. Not back East—whatever the job they might give you—even if they made you General of the Army."

"Maybe," he said. "It depends on what Janna Dupard says, and what Amanda thinks."

"Then it's settled."

"You seem confident about it," he said. "I know Amanda will forgive me. But Janna Dupard? Well, I'm not so sure."

But I was, and that's the way it happened.

CHAPTER 17

THE Serona gave me some credit for breaking up the charge that almost swept them through the village. I was installed in a hut with Levi and Brown Leaf, Christian's foster mother, to tend me. That brown, sturdy Indian woman didn't much resemble Mrs. Harper physically—distance and circumstance placed them far apart. But despite all that, they had certain traits in common. They could love the homeless and give care to those who needed it, whether deserved or not.

Levi made peace with himself for what he had done, as I knew he eventually would. He spent a day or so sincerely marveling at Janna Dupard's capacity to forgive. Secretly, that gave me a little hope.

However, I wasn't surprised when, on the second day, he told me Janna had asked him to take her and the boy out.

"I won't go if you think you'll need me here," he said.

"What about Janna?"

"She'll have to wait until you can ride."

"No, Levi. Do as she says."

"You sure that's what you want, Sax?"

"I'm sure."

"Where will you go when you leave here?"

"Maybe back to the Grand Wash Cliffs. I like it up there."

"You'll come back through Yuma. You promised Amanda a few days."

I wasn't sure I wanted to do that, but I had promised.

"Yes," I said.

"Well, there are things I must do to get ready," he said, rising.

"What about the boy, Levi?" I asked.

"What about him?"

"Well, what kind of boy is he?"

"He reminds me a lot of you when I first met you. Independent, though certainly not so headstrong. There is still time for him to learn that, though."

"I hope not, Levi."

"You mean to tell me a modicum of judgment has seeped into that head of yours?"

"I doubt it, Levi. And sometimes I wish it would."

"Me, too," he answered. "But then you wouldn't be Sax, would you?"

"Not this Sax anyway."

I wanted him to talk about the boy a little, but I didn't know how to ask.

Levi must have sensed that, because he said, "Would you like the boy to pay you a visit?"

The idea was tempting—tempting as all get-out. But I doubted Janna would allow it. The look on her face just before I faced off with Bustamente was still vivid in my mind, and the quick way she had disappeared with the boy.

"No. No, I don't think so," I said.

"He has asked me a lot of questions about you."

"What kind of questions?"

"About your past. Where you are from. That sort of thing."

"What did you tell him, Levi?"

"The truth, as far as I know it."

"I expect you killed what might have, under other circumstances, budded into a friendship."

"Maybe, but I doubt it. He still seems to have plenty of questions."

"Be best if you let his mother answer his questions about me from now on, Levi."

"If that's the way you want it, Sax."

He left then, and I lay there and thought about the boy. And about his mother, too. God knows, she was never out of my mind.

Sometime later I became aware that someone stood in the doorway. My first thought was Brown Leaf, who could enter that silently. I twisted for a look. It wasn't Brown Leaf. Christian Dupard stood there.

"I told Levi not to send you," I said, regretting the words before they were out—the gruffness of my voice as well.

"Colonel Piddington didn't send me," he said. He spoke quietly, deferentially. "I came on my own."

"Does your mother know you are here?"

"Which one? I have two, you know."

"I was thinking of the one from St. Louis."

"No, she does not know."

His English seemed to have come back to him. The little rusty hesitations were now gone. I guess that's the way it is when you speak a language until you are six. You never forget. It comes back instantly. That happens with a lot of things from one's youth, sometimes for the worse.

He was still dressed in Serona garb—a skirt-like garment that reached from his waist to just above his knees. He already showed the curvature of muscles in his arms and shoulders. His feet were bare, and they looked tough. The muscles in the calves of his legs looked developed. Somewhere the boy had learned to run. His hair was a light brown. It was cut straight around, reminding me of what some call a bowl cut. He had clear blue-gray eyes that contrasted startlingly with sun-browned skin. The Dupard hair and eyes? No wonder Janna had recognized him.

He looked me over just as carefully. I haven't felt that nervous since the first time I undressed before a woman.

"Do I pass muster?" I asked, a little jokingly. It seemed a dumb thing to say, but, as I said, I was nervous.

"You're awfully big," he said. "Was my papa as big as you?"

"Don't you remember your papa, Christian?"

"I remember him, and I think he was big."

"I'm sure he was, but I never knew him."

"If you didn't know him, why did you come after me?"

"Your mama didn't tell you?"

"She doesn't like to talk about you much."

"She hired me as a guide," I said.

"Thank you, then," he said.

There was something a little sad in his voice.

"Don't you want to go home, Christian?"

"Yes, but I hate to leave Brown Leaf and Toucan. I asked Mama if we could take them to St. Louis. She says they wouldn't like it there."

"Do you remember when the Apaches traded you to the Serona and you first came here, Christian?"

"Yes, I remember."

"Did you like it here then?"

"No, not as much as I do now. I wanted to go home."

"That's the way it would be with Toucan and Brown Leaf in St. Louis."

He thought about that for a moment. "I wouldn't want them to go then," he said.

"You'll be busy in St. Louis," I said. "You have a lot of catching up to do—a great many things to learn."

"There is one thing I would like to learn."

"What is that?"

"I would like to learn to shoot—like you do."

I didn't speak for a moment. What was there I could say, knowing his mother felt as she did. But skill with a gun is nothing to put down if it's used right. I might have stepped across the line at times. Levi was quick to tell me that. Some would say I had done it with Bustamente, and I think I did. On the other hand, we might never have reached the Serona. The redheaded renegade and his buddies could testify some to that.

"There are good ways and bad ways to use a gun, Christian."

"Yours are good, Mr. Younger."

He would hear differently about that, I told myself. Not wanting him to follow up on it, I changed the subject.

"Levi tells me you, your mother, and he will be leaving," I said.

"I don't know why we don't wait for you, Mr. Younger."

"Your grandfather is very sick, Christian. He wants to see you before he . . ."

"Before he dies. That's what Mama says."

"She's right. It'll mean a lot to your grandfather."

He got up to go. "Will we ever see you again, Mr. Younger?"

"I don't know, Christian. I turn up in strange places sometimes."

"Colonel Piddington says you live alone in the desert a lot."

"Yes. Yes, I do."

"Maybe you could visit St. Louis."

"I might. You never know."

"Will you come to see me if you do?"

"I'd like that, Christian."

"You promise?"

"I promise."

He left then. I felt more alone than I had for a long time.

Brown Leaf came and went. Levi dropped in to say they were about ready to leave.

"Until Yuma," he said.

"Until Yuma."

I kept listening for their horses to ride out. Then Janna Dupard stepped through the doorway. I pushed myself up despite the wound. She might have been paying a social call in St. Louis from her outward calm. But I had learned to read her eyes by then. They were dark now.

"How are you, Sax?" she asked.

"Healing," I said. "Healing fast."

"I came to say goodbye," she said.

"I know. I . . . I hoped you would."

"What did you think of Christian?"

"He told you he came to see me?"

"Yes."

"He's a fine boy, Janna. Maybe his three years out here were good."

"Maybe," she said, "but there are a lot of things in him I find strange."

"Such as?"

"Well, there's this gap. I don't know what happened to him. I don't know what it'll make him like."

"You might not know that had he been under your feet all his life."

"I suppose," she said. "I don't know you, either. I thought I was beginning to, but I don't."

"Is it important that you know me?"

"I thought it was . . . until you . . ."

"Until I shot it out with Bustamente."

"Yes," she said, but she turned her face away, as if she didn't want me to see something there.

"I told you once there was something in me I hoped you never saw."

"I saw it in your face just before you drew."

"I guess I was thinking of that, but there is probably more."

"More?"

I didn't answer. My soul had already been stripped a little bare. I didn't want her to see anymore. No, that's not quite right. I didn't want to see it myself, either.

"You may find a lot of me in Christian now, Janna."

I didn't plan to say that. The words just came out. Her face froze for an instant. She took control again, relaxing that look a little. The thought wasn't all that new to her, I decided.

"No," she said then.

There was finality in the word, as if she had set her will against it, and now was renewing the stand again.

"No, he will never be like that," she said then.

How many mothers have said that? How many have fought against it? I thought of my own mother. Would she have dropped me off that horse if she had known this was how I would be?

It was a draw—time to quit. We both knew it. She stood.

"Goodbye, Sax."

"Goodbye, Janna."

They left that day—Janna, Christian, Levi, and a Serona escort to see them part of the way. I lay there and thought of St. Louis. The Paris of the Prairie, some called it. I wondered if I would like it—that is, if I ever got up the nerve to go.

After a while, I pulled the two books I had brought along from my saddlebag, unwrapping them from the soft leather. I put the Good Book aside for later. I opened the volume of Shakespeare to *Othello*. Now, there was a man of action. Too quick to act at times—on one occasion, at least. I knew a little of how he must have felt.

If you have enjoyed this book and would like to receive details of other Walker Western titles, please write to:

Western Editor
Walker and Company
720 Fifth Avenue
New York, NY 10019

B-2

WESTERN   Pelham, Howard.
FICTION   Judas guns

89048377

JUL 1 0 1990

RODMAN PUBLIC LIBRARY
215 East Broadway
Alliance, OH   44601